For Kathleen
at the start of a
fine friendship
from Bibbi
April 1, 1991
Onlay, France

Nothing Grows by Moonlight

Torborg Nedreaas

Nothing Grows by Moonlight

Av måneskinn gror det ingenting

Translated by Bibbi Lee

University of Nebraska Press

Lincoln and London

Originally published as
Av måneskinn gror det ingenting,
© H. Aschehoug & Co.
(W. Nygaard) 1947, 1975
English translation
Copyright © 1987 by Bibbi Lee
All rights reserved
Manufactured in the
United States of America
The paper in this book meets the
minimum requirements of
American National Standard for
Information Sciences—
Permanence of Paper for
Printed Library Materials,
ANSI Z39.48–1984.
Designed by Dika Eckersley
Typeface: Schneidler,
Schneidler Medium, display
Typesetter: Composing Room of
Michigan, Inc.
Printer: Edwards Brothers
Library of Congress
Cataloging-in-Publication Data
Nedreaas, Torborg.
Nothing grows by moonlight.
(European women writers series)
Translation of:
Av måneskinn gror det ingenting.
I. Title. II. Series.
PT8950.N35A913   1987
839.8′2374   87-5000
ISBN 0-8032-3313-2 (alk. paper)

for Åse

I am looking for someone. I have been looking for this person for thirteen days now. I have crisscrossed the city in every direction. I have been through every hotel lobby, looking, searching. I have ridden the streetcar randomly, expecting, as a matter of course, to see that blue coat standing out among the passengers. I have been every place where people congregate, searching their faces, in case this one face should cross my path once more. But no. Perhaps I just want to look at those features for a moment, to

1

recognize them. We don't know each other's names. I just want to look at those features for a moment, sink into that human soul for a short second and take it with me. Look into the depths of a human soul, given to me one night by two grieving hands.

It is really very difficult to say what it was that made me notice her. It was probably many things, my own mood, the weather, the emptiness of that particular day. What do I know. Certain days are like that . . . empty. You ache inside and the day sets you apart and turns you away. And I was drifting, not wanting to go anywhere, not wanting to go home either. It was the kind of spring evening that brings a little rain, just enough rain that you notice tiny pinpricks on the sidewalks while the blue dusk stays mild and clear at the same time. The street lamps had just been turned on, blond candles jumping out into the blue half-light. It smelled of March evening and damp sidewalks. I drifted into the railroad station. I really had no business at the station, but I bought a newspaper at the newsstand to make it look as if I had a reason for being there.

It was then that I discovered her. Just as I was stuffing the newspaper in my pocket and turning around to leave, I noticed her standing there looking for someone, waiting for someone. Mother-of-pearl dusk was seeping through the glass roof above us while a yellow light from a lamp fell across her shoulders and her hair. Her head was bare. Her face was in the shadow. I didn't see any of it clearly.

Inside the station voices sounded like the singing blows from a hammer. All sounds were reverberating, enclosing us, shutting us in together. Perhaps that was what did it, and also this searching look of hers. I felt as if she was looking for me, or something; it's hard to say because she looked so perfectly ordinary and I didn't need a girl. I hadn't thought of any such adventure that evening. But I have to dwell a little on this because it is a particularly clear memory. I have to caress it a little and hold it closely, even though it may seem insignificant.

A young girl was standing there. I imagined her to be nineteen or twenty years old. A complete stranger to me, whose face I could not even see. She was standing there with a small red suitcase in her hand, looking as if she didn't know where to go. Her coat hung open and loose around her body. She had one hand in her pocket. The hand holding the suitcase was naked, without a glove. Smooth hair, flat shoes. I walked around her and came up behind her; she had bent her head a little. I spoke to the hair hanging softly down to her shoulders. There were no particular intentions on my part and I did not think about what I was saying at all, nor about having to say anything.

"Can I help you with anything, Miss?" The warmth in my voice surprised me a little; there was always the possibility of being turned down, and also that she might be a streetwalker. She shook her head slowly without turning to look at me; she wasn't even interested in turning around to see who was talking to her or to give me an icy stare. I still hadn't seen her face. I said, "I will carry your suitcase for you." She started walking then, her head bent. She walked toward the exit. I followed close behind. She stopped, as though she couldn't quite make up her mind. I said, "We'll take the other exit." And I walked past her without looking at her, knowing she was there, following on my heels. I noticed that her suitcase rattled a little; I sensed her breath, and the sound of her shoes right behind me felt intimate and close, as if she were whispering to me.

My thoughts were chaotic. Where were we going, what in the world was I going to do with this strange girl, who was she, how was she, what would be the end to this evening? Offhand I said, "Your place or mine?" She walked a moment before she answered. "Let's walk a little first," she said. I turned toward her then and allowed her to catch up with me. It was then that I first looked at her, seeing her face for the first time. And now I must dwell once more because there is something to this, seeing a person's face for the first time. You want to look back to that moment to find the connection with the next phase: the moment you see the person who owns this face, the real person. We were just walking toward a street lamp. It had become slightly darker. The light fell across her face, undressing it for me. Then we were past the lamp and her face returned to the shadows. It was as if she had hidden herself again. But during that short second while

3

the light fell across her features I noticed that she was considerably older than I had thought, in her late twenties, maybe closer to thirty. There was something childlike in her features, something yet to be experienced, but the fine lines around her eyes and a quite noticeable line running from the base of her nose had all taken their time to develop. She said, "Let's just walk around."

We walked in silence. Cars slid slowly past on the pavement, streetlights played with our shadows, swirling them around us. From time to time I looked at her; she was looking straight ahead, something darkly brooding in her eyes. Her mouth was large and blooming with sensitivity, but was without color, and it firmly shut over her thoughts. If she had any thoughts. I didn't know, maybe didn't even think about it. I was puzzled by the fact that I had no desire for her. But my heart beat uncomfortably. Her footsteps were whispering at me, and her proximity felt like an unsettling touch.

When you experience something, an event or a human being, that forces itself into your life, giving it meaning, you often notice the little things most. Everything that connects you with the experience, even the most inconsequential detail, takes on a life of its own and demands something of you. Here I was walking around the streets on a wet March evening with a strange girl. We didn't talk, I didn't know her name, but everything that happened burned into my consciousness and will always be a part of me, part of my deepest self. We were approaching the docks. I smelled the odor of the sea, and from where the fishing boats were anchored came the scream of a sea gull. I will always experience this powerful feeling again when I smell the odor of the sea, and I thought it strange to hear the scream of a sea gull in the evening. It was just one single scream. Then a car honked and a streetcar rattled by, screeching in its tracks. Her hair had become wet, sticking to her head. It was smoothed away from her forehead and hung straight down. Whenever the light hit it, it was yellow; otherwise it was ash blonde. Light and shadow fell across her as we walked. Her face slowly glowed, then receded into the shadows once more. We were approaching the old part of town. There were only a few gas street lamps, whose tentative light created phosphorescent zigzags among the rainsoaked cobblestones. The tiny houses were either in the middle of the street or hidden by a stump of a garden, without any order, without symmetry. They hid behind newer storage buildings and peeked out anxiously, their tiny windows filled with flowers, dozing in the light from the gas lights.

She came to a halt in front of one such little house and grabbed the iron fence that protected the remnants of its small garden. Her voice was warm, ripe with womanhood.

"I've always wanted to live in such a house," she said. "Such a tiny little house with curious windows and many flowers."

I said nothing. A certain mood emanated from what she was saying, from this small talk about clothes on a line and a tiny little house. Some people can talk about art or literature, or they can tell an interesting anecdote that you listen to, but none of it reaches more than your brain, your conscious mind. But this telling can also be done so that what is being said sneaks through your skin and lets you experience something with your innermost self. This girl was talking about clothes hanging out to dry and sunshine and a little house in a way that involved me. She created a mood that went to my blood and made me experience it. That's why I have to dwell and think about this; I have to live through it again because it opened a door into this person whom I did not know. When we approached the center of town once more, she almost imperceptibly crept closer to me. I didn't physically desire her. But I wished our walk would never end. Her shoulders touched my arm from time to time. It felt good. I didn't want her any closer.

There was a lit shop window with coils of rope inside, and fishing gear and heaps of handwoven nets. She stopped, her back to the window. She had this dark, brooding look in her eyes.

"You."

Just that one word. It lit a shining joy inside me. I didn't dare answer, didn't dare hear my own voice for fear of clouding up my joy. I listened.

"It's strange. But the way we are walking now feels good. I feel really good now."

There was no melancholy in her voice, and no joy. She just said it, stated it, without bewilderment. As we walked on she said, "God knows why that is. After all is said and done, that's probably the only thing we all long for. The warmth of another human being at our side."

She emphasized each word. Each word lay there, seething, after she stopped talking. I could feel my breath shaking.

I have difficulty finding words for what was happening. I experienced her sequentially. Again and again a door was opened, a door into a human soul. And each time I caught a glimpse of yet another part, hiding inside.

A human soul is something that only has meaning to those who also have a soul. A large segment of the human race has none. And those who have one take care not to display it. That's why the experience is so violent: being touched by what you call a human soul at the first meeting. And here I have to backtrack again; I have to look at this. I cannot easily let it go.

I met a girl who came along just like that. You can meet beautiful girls or girls whose rhythm awakens your desire, girls who come along. More often than not they talk; they talk and laugh and fool around. That's part and parcel. And here I'd met one; I didn't know whether or not she was beautiful. She was standing still in the railroad station with a small red suitcase in her hand, and she had no rhythm because she was standing still. And she didn't talk, nor did we agree on where we would go. I didn't have the faintest idea what I wanted with her. But I sensed her next to me the whole time. Something about her proximity made my skin tingle; something made me feel unsettled, making my heart beat with a mixture of anxiety and expectation, without desire. And then there was this silent communication between us as we walked, which made me aware of *the human being* walking alongside me. The human being in possession of a soul capable of absorbing pain and happiness and, above all, capable of all that fury of human pain which may kill someone or may maim even when happiness embraces it. That pain which shapes the human being and in time emanates from the skin, creating a strange attraction.

6

She didn't say anything when I stopped by my front door and unlocked it. She walked right in ahead of me. On the stairs she waited a moment, making room for me to pass, lightly touching my arm. "Do you have anything to drink?" she asked.

That question could have placed her in a bad light. Particularly if I hadn't known as much about her as I already did. The way things were, this question about something to drink brought out a tenderness in me, a slightly aching tenderness. The only thing I could do for her was to get her something to drink.

I had something, not a lot. But she was satisfied. "Lots of cigarettes?" she asked. "Enough cigarettes?"

Fortunately, I had a full supply of cigarettes.

She warded me off when I went to help her off with her coat. "Wait," she said. She was busy examining my bookcase.

Usually I can gauge my fellow human beings on the basis of what first interests them about my living room. Going for the bookcase often makes me suspicious. It could be pure affectation. But girls normally show their affectation by standing enraptured in front of a painting. They don't look at the French etchings. I would have imagined this girl to pick a book on philosophy or something to do with art history, to prove her breeding. Such things are only human. Her choice surprised me a little. She was turning the pages of the *Decameron*. A delicate little smile was playing with her mouth, but her eyes were still searching. I asked if she knew the book. She nodded, not taking her eyes off it. Her hands, busy with the book, were long and expressive. The fingers on her right hand were darkly stained by nicotine, and there was some stain on her left hand too. There was no ring, no jewelry. When she replaced the book I asked her how she liked it. She shrugged her shoulders.

"I liked it when I was young. I liked it when I thought love was something lighthearted and fun. It says 'love' where it should say 'making love'."

I asked if she didn't think it was just about the same thing. She looked at me then. "You know as well as I that lovemaking is pleasure and, often for me, happiness. And that love is rather, well, rather awful." She looked down, her voice reduced to a whisper. Then she grimaced and threw herself into a chair. She had not taken off her coat.

"I think we're getting solemn," she said.

It grated on my ears.

I poured; we drank in silence. I searched out her eyes; they slipped away. She smoked greedily. "Well," she said, and then she lifted her glass to me and drank from it in a way that made it look as if she wanted to have it over with. "You see," she said a while later, "I have to get a little tipsy." There was no sign of humor in her eyes. I felt uncomfortable with what she was thinking. I wanted to tell her not to be afraid. I really wasn't expecting anything of her other than her staying here in my living room and not leaving. The warmth of a fellow human being next to me . . . had she only known how much that meant. The only thing is, there are so few fellow human beings.

I heard her drag eagerly on the cigarette she was smoking. Her eyes were fastened on me, searching and without seduction. The furrow in her forehead was quite marked now. It struck me that she might be over thirty. But her figure was that of a young girl. Long girlish legs, one foot turned in a little. Under her coat she wore a gray sporty skirt and a pale blue shirt with a tie. The severe tie only served to make her features more childlike. She wasn't really pretty, only her mouth, which was beautiful.

She smoked thirstily. She consumed the cigarettes until she had to hold the butt between thumb and index finger in order to suck in the last drag. The clock was ticking on the mantelpiece. In the apartment above, the radio was on, playing bouncy accordion music that scratched at the walls. She had leaned back in the chair and closed her eyes.

"Don't you want to take off your coat?" I asked. She answered without opening her eyes, "I'm cold."

The light fell directly on her face. It was mostly marked by fatigue now that she was relaxing. Her mouth shook a little. "You know what I feel like doing tonight?" she said slowly. I bent toward her, taking her hand. It lay limply in mine.

"But I don't know if I can," she said. "I don't know if you want to." I gave her hand a gentle squeeze.

8

"Tonight I'd like to talk. But it would probably bore you." Her eyes were still closed, and by looking at her mouth I could hardly tell that she was saying anything at all. I kissed her hand lightly as could be and felt her fingers tighten ever so slightly around mine. She said, "Can I?" She opened her eyes; they were asking. I let go of her hand, lit a cigarette, leaned back. "I'm waiting," I said. A quick smile slid across her face. Her seriousness never left the depths of her gray-brown eyes. She moved forward to the edge of the chair. The hem of her coat was dripping on the rug. "But I have to have something more to drink," she said. "I have to get a little more tipsy. I've got to get rid of it, if you can take it. I've been silent for many years," she said. I asked how old she was and she told me that she was thirty-eight.

I poured a beer glass half full of aquavit and placed it in front of her. She lit a fresh cigarette with the butt of the old one, and drank. In the apartment upstairs the radio served up a xylophone solo. She started humming along to the clownish tune in a low, hoarse voice. Her shoulders swayed imperceptibly to the beat. Then she stopped to take a drink. She groaned slowly as she put down her glass. It was raining more heavily outside; the rain whistled in the street and gurgled in a gutter. "I'm waiting," I said.

She said, "Don't be in a hurry. Then I can't do it." She was humming again, looking at me; shades of seriousness and wickedness played in her eyes. "It takes time for me, you see," she said. "It takes time for me because I have to think it over, so that I won't lie. Because I don't want to lie anymore, or to be silent anymore. You see, I'm too used to lying."

Right. Just like everyone. We walk around lying to each other's face and straight to each other's soul. We walk around getting muddled and inwardly burdened by each other's and our own lies.

She was holding the glass in her hand and leaning back again, cigarette dangling from the corner of her mouth. Her skirt had slid up over one knee a little, a child's round knee. She was looking at me from under her half-closed eyelids. You could tell

9

she was slightly under the influence. She said, "Well, then. You'll get your chance. You may choose. You can have my body, or you can have my soul. You may choose."

"Since I can't have both, I'll choose your soul."

"My body is much more beautiful," she said. "I'm just warning you. Besides, I'll steal the whole night from you, if I start talking."

"Start. Please."

Her mouth shook once more; her voice was barely audible.

"I'm just a little afraid, you see. Because if I thought I knew you, well, you don't understand this. But if you look at the clock I'll die of shame. Well, no, it's not that way. I'm lying. But I can't say anything, you understand? Unless you receive it."

"Dear . . ."

"And you have to believe me. You must reckon with the fact that I'm acting a little. Acting as in a play. Yes? We all do. But sometimes we play ourselves; we must be allowed to play ourselves some time. I'm properly tipsy now." She laughed quite a deep laugh. "You don't know what you've let yourself in for, asking for my soul. Because it'll bother you, all this. I know you are like that. That's why I want to open up to you. It would be too bad if I bore you. It may be that I'm not a good storyteller, particularly when I'm telling the truth. Maybe you're expecting a continuous story. But then it wouldn't be *the truth*. Life isn't like that, a continuous story. Once in a while we think and thoughts move backward to retrieve those things which make us think in the first place, and that changes the sequences around. That's the way it is. I, for one, have to tell a story that way, if I say anything at all. And then there are the details. Little things that aren't . . . that aren't . . . well. But they have to be there. What has no significance for one person can be a deciding factor for another. And the strangest things have often been deciding factors for me. And they have to be included. Do you really want this?"

"Continue."

She moved forward again as if listening for something. Her eyes had disappeared, away from me, from the living room, away from space and time. Her cigarette dangled between her

10

fingers, smoking itself. Her voice was low.

"I don't know why I must suddenly talk. Oh well, maybe I know."

She laughed slowly. "It's an old truth that a person experiences his whole life at the moment of death. I don't know which day I'm going to die. It's not for certain that I'll take my own life. I haven't done it before, so it probably won't happen now either." She laughed again and put the glass to her mouth.

"But when you met me at the station I was on the edge of an abyss. You've pulled me away from that abyss a little. But it *is* there. It's really always there, for people like me. It's really just circumstantial whether or not we stumble and plunge or not." She leaned her head back, closing her eyes. Her throat made a beautiful arch. Her mouth formed deep shadows in the light from the lamp.

"It's really a banal story. It's just that it's never been told. It's the kind of thing that people carry around by themselves. The kind that poets never write about. Poets usually write about beautiful things. They make even sorrow and tragedy beautiful. Poets!"

Her mouth grimaced imperceptibly. "Poets . . . they're the dispensers of truth. Often they tell the truth . . . part of the truth. They keep quiet about the rest or else nobody would buy their work. But what they hold back becomes the lie about the truth that they tell." She opened her eyes. "Do you understand this? It doesn't matter, anyway. I'm tipsy. That's nice. And now I want to talk, even if you fall asleep from it all. How far did I get? Oh, well, it doesn't matter. I hadn't even started. Cheers! Well, the story isn't original. It's about lovesickness and money problems and eroticism and adultery and the devil and his grandmother. Cheers to you! Do you have a match? Thanks. But listen now, don't look at the clock, you have to be awake, 'cause I want to see you pale. My story is about blood. Not poetic blood with beauty in it. No. Ugly. Awful. Blood and slime and pus. Yes? You're screwing up your forehead. I told you it wouldn't be beautiful. Because it's the *truth* what I'm about to say. Deceit and lies and hypocrisy, that's what the truth is. I've read quite a bit, but I have yet to read anything completely truthful. Except for medical books, and even they are incomplete. Oh, do you have another drink? I've gotten talkative. But I have to. And you have to put up with my thoughts. I have to get rid of all that I've been thinking about for so many years."

She took a few quick intense drags of her cigarette.

"Well, you see, once upon a time I became fond of a man. I was fifteen years old then and had just finished junior high school. Girlish infatuation! I was seventeen by the time it developed into something more. Because he was an upstanding citizen in the small town where I came from and, despite everything, he still is. He even sits in the municipal government; damned capable guy, you see. I can thank him for the *A* I got in all my exams. He was my teacher, you see. We had him for physics and math and English. And he was so important that I stretched, threw myself into those subjects during junior high school, even though he never tested me. Afterwards, when school was over, my hands started sweating every time I met him. Many little things like that happened; I clowned and spoke loudly and frantically with my girl friends whenever he walked by. Girlish infatuation?

"Well, girls are not so innocent in their infatuation as you might think. Poets write lots of beautiful things about what girls dream about. Well . . . *that* too. Just as much of it is not beautiful. Sweet little girls think lasciviously of obscene things. The worse, the better. Usually there is no real live object for the thoughts; no, it's all too secret for that. Even in their dreams they don't want any witnesses. I, for my part, dreamt about a real big, ugly, awful troll that wanted to bring me into his mountain cave to do unbelievable things to me. Or I dreamed about the devil. Especially when I was taking confirmation lessons from the minister.

"He told us to fear the devil and all his doings and all his being. Good Lord, how that fueled my imagination, this stuff about his being. I wanted nothing more than to become acquainted with this fantastic devil. But my answer on confirmation day was a promise to fear him. Everybody did. And everybody lied.

"That's the first official lie we become guilty of. According to

12

old custom, you don't enter the adult ranks without lying in front of the altar. That is the initiation. Society demands this lie from us over sacramental wine. Isn't it fantastic? I'm not making any sense. Cheers, there!"

She emptied her glass. I was turning mine around between my fingers.

◑

She'd become quite inebriated; she spilled ashes on the tabletop whenever she flicked the cigarette across the ashtray. She was humming and laughing. Suddenly she grabbed her face with both hands and groaned.

"Oh God, it's too awful. Everything is too awful. Once in a while there is a vacuum in my drunkenness, and then it's more awful than ever. I almost want to cry. But when I cry it's like the scream of a deaf-mute. Well, shoot, seems like I'm good and drunk anyway."

She laughed a little.

"This must be god-awful boring to you. Well, I assume you're telling the truth. Love, well. There should be no name for it. Because it is . . . well, it's not something you can put a name on. Some of the murkiness that lives its bacterialike existence in a young girls fantasy is mixed up in it. No, I'm lying. The murkiness has more profound causes, of course. I'll leave that to psychoanalysts to mess with. But then a man arrives, a real live man, and he's been there the whole time. Some are stuck on movie stars during that period, some on sports idols, but those of us who are basically faithful continue to build on our childhood infatuation. Caress it maybe, nourish and cultivate and all the stuff we do to explain the facts. All right by me. The result is the same anyway and people have tied this unwieldy concept to the word *love*. It has to do with happiness—no, I can't explain it. It's just that you get so unreasonably happy and shiny inside with one specific person."

She was talking more confidently. She was immersed in her own perceptions and less concerned with how it was affecting me. Her eyes had a distant glow and her cheeks were blushing.

"Why? Well, I mean why just this one person. Some people can tell you why they love such and such a person, but then there's something wrong. It's admiration then, or sympathy, or something you're impressed by. Love is something quite different. Not eroticism either—yes, you're looking at me. Well, well, well, let it be erotic then, but in that case eroticism is not what we all walk around thinking it is. Eroticism is something quite disembodied then. Other men have been more erotically profitable for me than he has. But no one has made me blossom, made my soul blossom, other than he. And why?

"He's not any more handsome than others, quite the contrary. Not tall; no more intelligent than other school teachers. No more intelligent than the others in municipal government.

"Not tall. He wasn't tall, I don't just mean physically. He was . . . well, he still is . . . just as limited, just . . . oh well, it doesn't matter. He was like most well-regarded citizens. Oh God, well, I don't know. Sometimes I think he proved himself bigger; oh yes, I'll tell you . . . he was wonderful. And he's more intelligent than most. Yes, he's fantastically intelligent. I'm the one who's too stupid to judge him properly. Remember that whenever I say something derogatory about him, remember that it's because I'm sometimes a little bitter toward him, a little angry with him.

"Well, I have been angry with him sometimes. I almost killed him a couple of weeks ago. I had an irrepressible urge to kill him. You see, he was lying next to me, his head back slightly, his mouth open. He was snoring. But his throat was tense; I could see his pulse beating. And I thought that just a small pocketknife would suffice for this artery and he would never awaken again.

"This is true, you understand. I would have killed him, I'm capable of such things. His glasses saved him. It happened when I went to take the knife out of his vest pocket. His glasses were in his vest pocket too and I happened to hold them for a moment, look at them for a moment . . . no, no, no, this has nothing to do with the real thing; I'll get back to it later. In a long, long, time.

"I'm probably prattling a lot, but you have to allow me. I can't tell it any other way, and you mustn't look at the clock. I can't allow what I'm telling to bore anyone because it would all fall apart for me then. I'm drunk now, you see, but I have to be drunk to be able to tell the truth; I'm too used to lying. Well, let's have a toast. You have to look after me so I don't get too drunk. I'm afraid. Oh God, how I'm afraid sometimes. It'll pass, and tonight I must talk. Where was I? I think I have to backtrack. No, you mustn't expect continuity; the red thread got tangled long ago. Tell me, did you ever hear of women who chased married men? The fact is that it's always the woman who's responsible when a man cheats on his wife. The woman that he cheats her with.

Well, she probably deserves it. Well, does she? I'll get back to that later. There's something wrong there, see. Something terribly wrong. Inviolate marriage!"

She took a few petulant drags on her cigarette. "I've been married myself, I'll tell you. WHOA!" I jumped to. She was leaning back, laughing.

"I scared you but good now. Well, it's this thing about the inviolate sacred marriage. Listen to this, I chased a married man. He got married when I was eighteen. I wanted him myself, wanted his children. I was seventeen the first time he had me. He was already engaged, but I didn't know it. There's something I have to tell you first—it's about our town. There are laws at work all over the world, but a town like ours has its own laws. It's a kind of spin-off from those other laws, a caricature of those other laws. The general hypocrisy that is tolerated elsewhere in the world is the accepted religion in our town. A teacher is usually decent everywhere, but in our town he's several degrees more decent.

"Let's say he's been on a trip to The Mine, which is located a few kilometers above town, and that he's met a girl there who's been a student of his. She's the daughter of an ordinary mineworker up there, but she's done well in school and graduated with the best grades. It's probably permissible for him to show enough interest in such a good student to ask her if she wants to continue, if she wants to become a university student. He has even arrived with another teacher, and there's nothing wrong in his talking to the girl who has seen him from her window and fabricated an errand for herself.

"That's the kind of girl I was. I even brought a magazine along, an English periodical with a poem in it that I wanted to translate to make a few coins. And I was breathless with nervousness 'cause if he'd thought about it he would have found it pretty strange, my taking a walk with an English magazine. And then I showed him the magazine with the poem. All three of us sat down on a rock in the sunshine. Along the edge of the road there were tiny daisies that I pulled up and tore apart. And I talked and talked about that poem and asked questions I already knew the answers to, to make him stay a few minutes more, to make us sit there as long as possible. He found his glasses and studied the poem, and I found other things in the magazine that I asked him to read just to make him sit right next to me for a while.

"But then they didn't want to sit there anymore; they were going back down and told me goodbye. And now you'll hear something funny: a while later he came up looking pretty anxious. He was looking for his glasses. He was sure he'd left them on the rock. Lucky for him, don't you think, that I arrived just at that moment. I'd been for a short walk in the forest to pick some white wood anemones and had just returned to the rock at the side of the road as he was about to leave because his glasses weren't there. Because I'd found them and kept them, so there!

"He thanked me, saying that was wonderful. You should have seen him smile there in the sunlight. He was young then, and hot from the sun and the walk, and he didn't wear a hat, even though it was Sunday. And he probably had no idea exactly how thoughtful I'd been. If the truth be known, I'd kept his glasses even before he and the other teacher left. Well, he'd been careless enough to put his glasses down on the rock, and I put the magazine on top of them and sat there with my heart beating wildly, not hearing a word they were saying. The only thing I heard was my heart saying 'don't take the glasses, don't take the glasses, don't take the glasses' . . . and he left without the glasses. Oh God, those glasses!

"No, I'm not crying at all, just some smoke in my eyes, well, cheers there! This must be terribly boring for you to listen to. Is there any more liquor? I'd be happy with some red wine. I'm going to drink everything you've got in the house and when it's all gone I'll get boring and you can shoo me out. Is it boring about glasses? Well, I have to include such things.

"These glasses, you see, they gave me as much happiness in the course of three-quarters of an hour as other people experience in a week. Just about. I hid in the forest and put them on and noticed that everything turned dizzy and uncertain and totally meaningless when I looked through them. Then I took them off and blinked to regain my normal vision. Then I stroked them, patted them as carefully as you pat a baby bird, and had some of those feelings you have when you hold a baby bird in your hand. And I kissed them, the glass, the stems, the nosepads I kissed. And I lay down in the moss with the glasses on and closed my eyes and folded my hands across my chest while holding a few wild white anemones, and I pretended I was dead and took his glasses along in death—no, I'm making a terrible mess of this. 'Cause I really don't remember what I pretended or thought at all; I just remember lying there with his glasses on my nose and that I was happy to be wearing his glasses. What are you laughing at?

"For God's sake, don't laugh at this just because it sounds a little messed up. It's serious to me. And I hid them on my chest, on my bare skin. No, you don't understand this. But I was on my way to town that day too, with the white anemones for my girl friend. Just then, as he was going back down. You understand? And I knew about a beautiful shortcut through the woods.

"So, so, so, I don't want to talk about this. I can't recount this without it falling apart for me. Because it isn't just like so, good or bad or something with a label. A terrible happiness in my soul and an unbelievable disappointment . . . no. What am I prattling on about? I think I'm drunk. Give me another glass of red wine, if you please. No, I'm not crying. Are you crazy? That would be complete madness. This is more than twenty years ago, isn't that funny?

"But you should have seen his smile when he got his glasses back; I wish you could have seen his smile. He's ugly, you know. Well, not ugly, not really, he just has a messy face. I often had fun combing his eyebrows with my pocket comb; I've combed them upward and made him look like a devil and I've combed them down over his eyes, making him look like a gloomy forest troll. And his nose is completely impossible, absolutely, hopelessly impossible. But his smile cannot be matched by anyone. Can you imagine? That a human being can smile so that the whole world glitters and your whole insides are filled with trembling sunspots?"

She was silent. Her mouth closed around a little smile and her eyes stared, pale and dreamy, at something inside her. The radio upstairs had quieted down; there were footsteps across the floor. The rain trickled peacefully in the gutter outside, and a solitary car sputtered on the wet pavement.

◐

I don't know how long we sat there like that, silent and not moving, but I think I almost fell asleep with my eyes wide open. Dizzy shadows from sunspeckled young birch forests and a fragrant blanket of white anemones danced around in my brain, interwoven with a picture of a young girl lying on her back, with anemones in her folded hands. And glasses on her nose. I smelled the fragrance of wild white anemones and the forest floor. Then I heard her voice again. This warm womanly voice that so completely drew me into an existence far outside my well-known living room.

"Such a small town. It shapes its people, dictates their character, terrorizes every single individual. You'd think a person was a person and that he'd be the same, wherever he ended up, right? You know they say that your character is your destiny. You might add that environment is character. The environment in a larger town is sufficiently varied so that people have the space to be different from one another. While such a small place . . . oh.

"The people there are like some kind of oatmeal soup. Yes, that's it, they're a particular kind of oatmeal soup, and woe to the one who comes there as anything but a grain of oats. You may laugh. But that's the way it is. My big mistake, you see, my mistake from the very first moment is that I'm no grain of oats. Were I a prune or a raisin I might have been tolerated in the oatmeal soup. But, you see, I'm a peppercorn. It wouldn't matter how much I tried to look like a grain of oats, you can taste a peppercorn right away and then all the other grains of oats would wrinkle up their noses, not wanting any kind of spice in their soup."

She laughed; she was really having a good time with her comparison, and I saw how beautiful she must be when she was happy. She lit a cigarette with pleasure. She slowly blew out the match. It looked as if she was quite slowly kissing the flame until it died. She said:

"Imagine a hedge. A long row of trees planted next to one another, made up of all the kinds of trees we know here at home, pine and fir and alder and birch and all the others. All mixed up. But all of them pruned and cut exactly the same so that they make a continuous plane all along. Then suddenly a tree is planted that no one knows, of a kind that doesn't normally grow in those parts. And suddenly the pruning shears don't cut properly; that tree cannot be shaped the same way as the others in the hedge. Then they start to saw and hack away to make the tree like the others. They ruin the bark and ruin the pith, but it still isn't like the other trees. Imagine that! This is stupid. And I got away from what I was thinking about.

"But *he* was a fine tree at any rate, an aspen. That's what he was, an aspen with a solid trunk and the kind of leaves that shake when you blow on them. But he let himself be pruned and looked like one of the other trees in the hedge. But innermost he was an aspen.

"And when we came out on the country road once more he told me to wait for a while and to come down by myself—we should walk separately. I don't know if you'll understand any of this. First *that,* in the forest. My hair smelled of the forest floor, my dress too. And I was still shaking from what had just happened, and I was full of confusion, happiness, and fear and tenderness and shame, and then pain, the disappointment—well, I just don't know. It isn't so easy to really explain what happens to a girl, the first time. But if he'd hit me straight in the face . . . no. I can't explain. This thing back on the road. When he suddenly turned into the town teacher again, when he wanted to walk back down alone, wanted us to walk separately. You understand, I've excused him for twenty years. But then again he was a teacher in a small town; he held a vulnerable position. Besides, he was engaged, but I didn't know that then. And my dress was wrinkled; to tell the truth, it was quite wrinkled. Of course he was right; in such a situation it was right to walk separately. But . . . oh. This is difficult. Please be patient with me."

She smoked greedily for a while. Her eyes searched steadily inward for words. I could feel my heart pushing each beat against my rib cage.

"The pain, you understand. It was so unexpected, the fact that it hurt so much. I didn't know that, didn't know that it would hurt that much. But there's happiness in that too. A tender, devotional feeling of happiness. Otherwise everything in me was a shambles, modesty, shame . . . oh, but it was so long ago. At any rate, I needed not to be walking alone just then. Or maybe it would have been better if he'd just said that I'd lost the flowers for my girl friend, I'd better find some new ones, he'd better hurry on down . . . he could have said that, for example, and things would have been better for me. Do you understand this? Thank you—oh God, how you're understanding. You're nice.

"My God, how young girls are stupid—yes, how women are stupid, almost their whole lives. He said, 'I love you.' He said, 'There's only the two of us, just you and me.' And he whispered my name and I never knew I had such a beautiful name. Well, you know all this. You know you always say these things, just at that moment, and afterwards. But he'd said it to me, who'd never heard it before, who'd maybe dreamed about hearing it from him, even. And he'd said it in the birch forest, just a little while ago, and I still felt the breath of his heated words in my ear . . . and then. And then this. On the country road. Do you understand this—oh, but do you understand this?

"I was alone picking anemones, crying into the anemones. No, I think I'm lying, 'cause I can't really remember if I cried, but I can imagine that I cried. I can still feel my cheeks burning, but I'm not sure that I cried.

"All spring long I waited for him to call me. I had a little office job at The Mine; he could have called.

"Have you ever experienced spring . . . from the wrong side?" she slowly asked. "I mean . . . have you ever felt how malicious spring can be toward someone in pain? In the morning, early, early in the morning, birds start singing. Just a single one at first, while it's still night. You can hear it celebrating out there; the night is mother-of-pearl and blood. And the silence whispers, it whispers and buzzes of love and happiness; only it's not for you. There's sparkle and whistle in a bird's voice, but also crying. It is so beautiful and it feels like a burning scorn to your loneliness. Everything beautiful is sometimes horrible. Spring has almost always been horrible for me. As a rule I can only stand it when it rains. I like fall the best. There's something cool and soothing about it. Fall is the best time for the lonely."

She was silent. And I was silent. The rain crackled a little against the windowpane. Upstairs a door opened and closed.

"Before it happened, before that Sunday in the forest, I was alive with joy when spring came, when spring was the way you know it can be. Full of echoes of birdsong in the hills in the mornings, a riot of all kinds of birds in the morning, and then that wonderful, expectant stillness before everything wakes up. It is as if the birds hold their breath for a while and listen for the day. Then a cock crows in the hen house . . . that was something! When everything was just dreams and expectations. Well, it's hard to believe. The same things that sometimes make you vibrate with happiness can almost kill you at other times. Do you think this is drunk talk? It isn't, you know. Even though I wouldn't be able to talk this way if I hadn't had something to drink.

"Do you want to drink a toast with me? Pour something for yourself too. Sometimes I feel like we've known each other forever. It's just a mood, of course. But it could also be because you're a bit of me and I'm a bit of you. Well, that was a dumb thing to say. Cheers, then. You can like me and be my friend just this one night. I would like that and not . . . not anything more."

Her glass was empty. She sat there stroking the stem, slowly and thoughtfully. There was such expressive tenderness in her fingers it made my wrists shiver with cold.

"But it's true," she said, "he could have called. Or he could have written to me, just a small letter to say something or other. That I shouldn't worry or something. He could have asked how I was, just a formality. The switchboard lady needn't have understood anything. We have this switchboard, you see. A small place. Not really a town even. Because then I could have thought that at least he was thinking about me, that he would like to know how I was, but that he was afraid someone would understand something.

"Well, well, such a spring passes too and it has its good moments from time to time, moments that don't ache. Gray, rain-soaked nights. Muddy roads and waterlogged forest floors and birds that stop singing. Just an intermittent whistle from the hills at dusk. There's solace in that. A songbird whistling by itself in the rain is a sad little bird without a mate. It's complaining. Makes me think I'm not the only one who's lonesome. Well then, what was I about to say—oh yes.

"Up there at The Mine we have a theater. Saturdays and Sundays there's a movie up there and people from town often come up. And one day he came. Well. Well, no, it's nothing. But I'll see if I can tell it anyway. I need another drink, though.

"You'll think I'm terribly stupid. Every once in a while you do stupid things. Sometimes you do exactly what you shouldn't. Once I stood outside his window at night even though I didn't want to know what I came to know then. It almost killed me. That time I did exactly what I deep down knew I mustn't do under any circumstances. And then I did it anyway, even though I knew it would kill me. Yes, we do get killed a few times in our lives, you know. But this wasn't what I wanted to tell. This was much later.

"It was really about this evening at the movies. It wasn't raining then. The sky was made of cast metal. The hills, the roads, the mountain outcroppings held a thousand shades of gray—that's the way it sometimes is up there at home. Dusk shines like pale silver on such an evening, and nothing happened other than that he came to go to the movies and that this peaceful dusk with its warm gray colors and silver light in the mud puddles immediately became more delicious and beautiful than all the sunshine and all the colors in the world. Everything happens outside the theater, really, up there. Seeing who's there, talking to people a bit. Many people go to the movies just for the chance to dress up a little and meet people. We sit on the outcropping or hang around the outside of the youth center; it's almost sad when the performance starts.

"I was wearing a new suit that evening—well, not new, I had altered it, but it felt new, it looked nice. And he looked nice and well groomed in his blue suit, and I knew he was looking for me.

"Happiness can light up so quietly, it can embrace you so gently, and then all is well. Do you have any idea what that means? You stand there knowing little by little that all is well. I was standing there watching him turn away from the person he was talking to, letting his eyes rest on me and light up—they'd found their destination. I was standing there feeling that all was well.

"I must rest a little here. I must think about it for a while. It was a good moment. I sat behind him at the movie and felt good. It is so rare that you just feel good. Happy . . . happy? Oh. Happiness can often wear you out; you're so happy you get sick and tired of it all. I've been completely ill with happiness sometimes. But there at the movie, he sat right in front of me. I leaned forward to be close to him and I thought I could feel his neck and his hair breathe. He tingled in my skin.

"That's all. There wasn't any more than that. Maybe it's nothing? But I did tell you this would be nothing. An ordinary love story."

Suddenly she pushed her glass away and got up. Her voice was loud and reckless.

"No. I don't want to anymore. Yes, there's more, but I don't want to tell it."

She took a few steps across the floor, frantically intertwining her fingers.

"Why am I telling all this? You don't know me, you're bored. Oh God, how can I tell this story when it bores someone. It mustn't, don't you understand that this mustn't fall on the floor. It's something I hold in my hand and breathe on because I want to kiss it, but it can't stand to be kissed. And it certainly can't stand falling on the floor."

I said, "For God's sake. For God's sake, dear." She looked at me; it got so quiet for a while.

"I just don't know," she said quietly. "I really don't know you. But it's probably easier. Giving to a stranger that which is most difficult. To a complete stranger."

She came over and moved my hand away from my eyes. I straightened up. She was standing at a worried distance touching my hand ever so lightly. She had to stretch her arm out all the way, and immediately let go of my hand.

"You mustn't sit like that. It makes me think you're asleep. Well, I don't really think so, of course, but you never know. You mustn't be sleepy, and you mustn't be bored. Give me a cigarette. Thank you very much. Give me a little time. Then I'll tell you, but it'll be the way it happens, no continuity."

She walked back and forth across the floor, smoking, one hand in her coat pocket. She talked now to the bookcase, now to herself. She spoke to the pictures on the wall and the furniture in the living room and from time to time she picked up a vase or a small sculpture and held it in her hand, looking at it without seeing.

"Lots of things are interesting, we experience things that are full of action and decisions and full of change and everything. But what we remember best is what happens inside. Good little moments, quiet and full of happiness—or something painful that happens inside. And that evening at the movie, then, then, then. I don't want to mess around with this so much. No.

"But afterwards there was just fear. Such a moment makes you so deathly afraid after a while, because it ends so soon. Lots of people outside, he with his. I with mine. Girl friends and silliness—they mess around talking about the movie while they look at the boys. And every time I looked in his direction, he was looking at me. With a quick, warm smile in his eyes, you know. But he was talking to someone. My girl friends started moving toward the road, and he just stood there. I had to go along with the others. But I was nervous and everything was awful, so I left. I disappeared in peace and quiet and took a shortcut to intercept him. And this . . . well, this is the kind of thing one doesn't do, shouldn't do.

"I was sitting at the edge of the road looking at all the people coming around the turn in the road on their way back to town. I was in a fever. I thought, the next one will be him, no, but the next one; no, when three more have passed it will be him. And there he was."

She paused and took a few passionate drags on her cigarette.

"Suddenly, there he was. And I got up—no, I don't quite remember, but, yes, I must have gotten up because I remember having difficulties with my hands; I didn't know where to put them. I think they were fiddling with my jacket buttons near my throat. I glowed at him. I was in a fever. And his eyes were the way they were supposed to be as soon as he saw me.

"It had become darker, but the darkness was like silver and there were no stars. I was a star. Well, don't laugh. Because I felt I was a star moving toward him in the road. Don't laugh at this; there's no other way I can describe it.

"Have you noticed how a star sometimes shivers before it dies out behind a cloud? I was quite numb afterwards, after his cool greeting as he passed. He walked straight past me! Hurried up—suddenly his eyes had a grudging look, barely glancing at me—hurrying on. Then I felt nothing any more; I was numb all over. Black, black . . . the kind of black that comes when a star dies out behind a cloud."

Greedily she sucked in the last of her cigarette. Her voice was rough and low.

"There were other people in the road, you see."

She put the cigarette out carefully and used it to mess around with the ashes.

"He called the day afterwards. It was the teacher who called. But I lost my voice from sheer happiness and could barely answer. Something about a translation, or maybe it was something entirely different; I was so confused I cannot remember. His place, I was going to his place! He said six o'clock, or was it seven? In any case, I was in town before five, drifting, now at the docks, then in the streets. The clock seemed never to turn six or seven or whatever it was. I went to the cafe and ordered a soda, but I left the soda in a panic, thinking I'd be late. And then I drifted some more, beside myself with anticipation, and knocked on his door, fifteen minutes early.

"He was in his shirt-sleeves; he'd just shaved. He was a little shy and pulled on his jacket. I could have cried. Apologizing, he was apologizing to me! Because he'd been in his shirt-sleeves.

"And he'd set the coffee table. He bustled about getting the coffeepot, and then it turned out he'd forgotten to put in the coffee."

She laughed nervously, tapping her fingertips on her chin.

"But coffee was served at long last. We didn't drink it, though. It sat on the table getting cold. Well, later on in the night we drank coffee, we drank cold coffee and he smoked. I watched him smoke and every once in a while I'd take a puff, but it didn't taste good, it made me sneeze. And then it made us laugh and then we kissed each other until we were dizzy with craziness once more . . ."

She interrupted herself. She was standing still, looking down, both hands in her coat pockets.

"It was daylight when I went home. He didn't come with me. There was such an emptiness around my skin that I could feel every breath of air, and I was so vulnerable I got cold. But anyway."

She started wandering around again, her eyes still on the floor and her hands in her pockets.

"I remember once, when my sister was going to have a baby. There was endless consternation at home, quarreling and trouble. Well, she got married and everything was all right, but that wasn't until later. She would cry at night, so I'd crawl into her bed. At first she didn't want me to. She was angry because she was desperate, but mostly she was shy, I think. That fat stomach, you know. But I put my arms around her; I think I was a little shy too. But I couldn't avoid that big stomach—my sister was quite big right from the beginning. My nightgown was quite thin, and it was really strange, you know. There was something living inside her and I could feel it all the way through to my back. And even though I was really ashamed and shy I pressed close to her; I held my breath and really listened for what was happening. Because something was happening to me at that moment. What it was I couldn't possibly tell you. But afterwards, back in my own bed, there it came, that empty feeling around my own body. What am I rambling about? This is a whole different story; it really has nothing to do with anything. It's just that my body felt so meaningless. Nothing lived inside it."

She lit another cigarette and threw herself down on the armrest of her chair. She smoked almost half of the cigarette with audible drags before she continued. The furrow in her forehead was sharp and clear.

"There was that morning when I walked home. Well. It was really nothing, even so it was more than what had preceded it. He couldn't come with me, you see. Such a transparent little place what with one thing or the other. And my skin felt empty and meaningless; still, it was wonderful. Because he was still inside of me. I hurt, hurt just a little from him. Well, do you understand this? It was that time of year when the birds have finished singing; they just coo and chatter. They live inside the foliage and are terribly busy. I was singing a bit on my way, humming a little to myself and being happy. Because everything was so beautiful. The sun had to break through a purple wall of morning fog and that wall had a golden edge at first and the smaller clouds turned to gold for a while. And everything green woke up and became even greener, and the blue lake below The

Mine became a blue explosion just before the sun came out and transformed it to molten gold. Whenever a small breeze came across the surface, the lake boiled with gold."

She got up again and paced the floor. I got up too and she stopped to watch me, guardedly. I said I wanted to put some water on for coffee and she just nodded and paced the floor again. I ran the water and turned on the burner and before I went back in the living room I could hear a few tinkling sounds, brittle, from a music box. I had to gather myself together a bit; I was breathing heavily. Then I went back in.

She was standing with her head bent so that her hair was sliding down her cheeks. I couldn't see any part of her face. She'd found it—well, it wasn't particularly well hidden, not so well hidden that I couldn't bring it out to look at, turn it around in my hands and carefully put it back. But I never played it, never. But she played it. She turned the handle slowly around so that the tiny polka sounds popped out like shiny drops. It was a well-known simple little polka tune, a lively children's song, tremulously manufactured inside the music box. It came like shiny tears as she turned it. There she stood, playing and listening. Then she took a peek at me, sideways, almost without turning her head. A few notes still dripped at long intervals. She looked at me the whole time; I could feel it. Then she quit. Pling. She was holding the music box closely, her fingers stroking it carefully. She put it away tenderly, as if she was afraid of making noise, and looked at me, but immediately looked away. She didn't ask, thank God she didn't ask, about anything. It got so quiet. The stupid little tune was clinking inside my head, inside my heart.

She whispered, "Are you going to see if the water is boiling now?" Then I had to get out again, which was nice; it felt cooling. I made coffee, busily preoccupied. She didn't offer to help when I brought the coffeepot in, two cups threaded onto my finger and the creamer under my arm. She was turning the pages of some magazines and didn't look at me. She said, "It would be easier if you'd put everything on a tray or something." I was grateful to her for not being domestic and wanting to help. She wasn't a busybody the way so many people are. She just pushed the ashtray aside when I almost put the creamer on it. A long time passed before she said anything. She just sat there, distractedly blowing down into her coffee cup.

"I did tell you about the first time at his place, didn't I? Well. He went on vacation during the summer. But oh, I'm skipping, I have to include this. Shoot, I don't know where to start; there was so much that summer.

"First of all, my sister—she had a sweetheart and stayed out half the night. Me, I didn't have any sweetheart. You may well look at me. I was sitting in the bookkeeping office up there at The Mine doing bad work because all I did was listen for the telephone. Every time the phone rang in the boss's office I stopped breathing, my heart stopped and all my bloodcells stopped, and every living thing in me stopped to listen. Then when it turned out to be something else and the boss spoke on the telephone about oil and nails and screwdrivers, my heart started beating again along with everything else, but only to hurt me. The sun shone through the windows and the office was like an oven, but my brain was a lump of ice and my fingers were so cold I could barely write. Well, this is no story, no event. But when such things happen many times each day, every day for many weeks, something is happening anyway.

"And at home there was my sister. I hated her at that time because she would come home warm and happy, and because she sang while she worked. When that boyfriend of hers would whistle for her in the evening, I hated her. They didn't like the boy at home, so there was scolding. She sometimes cried in her room and she expected me to take her side and comfort her, but I said nothing. I was cold as ice and couldn't say a word to her. I turned my back on her and looked out the window, hating her because I would rather have cried her tears than freeze in my own coldness.

"It was impossible at home because I was so alone and couldn't manage to work or read, so I'd walk down the road, hoping someone from town was taking a walk. But only young people walked there, girls and boys and those who didn't directly belong to one another. They were full of happy expectations and were fooling around, warm and young. So there I walked among them, like something hunted, and I felt old and frozen. Being so lonely was a shameful thing, you know.

"Then I was hunted all the way back home. Even the nice weather and the forest and the rock outcroppings and the road turned me away. The beautiful old fir trees and the new forest by the lake were full of happy little secrets that were hidden from me and that didn't concern me. Can you imagine the evening sun blushing in the treetops and nature turning its back on you so you won't hear what it's whispering about?"

She had placed the little red suitcase on her lap and opened it. It made a rumbling sound; there wasn't much in it. She found a small container and took two little pills that she downed with coffee.

"Then I couldn't stand it any more. One day I couldn't stand it any more; I had to do something, had to straighten things out a little. Anything, no matter what, was better than the way things were. And then I went to his place one evening."

She slowly closed the suitcase. It looked as if her fingers barely touched the lock, and her hands rested on the red oilcloth as if she'd forgotten them.

"He wasn't home. But the landlady appeared in the upstairs window and said he'd gone to the pharmacist's. At first I was just disappointed at not finding him; it had cost me such a lot to get there. Initially, I didn't think about anything else. But then I drifted around, pretending I was taking a letter down to the pier and pretending I was studying the movie posters at the tobacconist's. Then I slowly started thinking and a small fear got more and more dense inside me, the kind of fear that lies like a cold lump under your diaphragm. The fact was that the pharmacist had a daughter. And I wanted the lump to go away and thought that it was possible for him to go to the pharmacist without that fact having anything to do with the daughter, right? But the lump just moved over and immediately came back and I tried to think of every other possible thing. When he came back everything would be all right.

"Well, I was waiting to intercept him. I was standing in a place where no one could see me from their windows and, besides, it wouldn't have mattered very much if anyone had seen me because I was thinking that anything would be better than the way things were. And then he came."

She took a cigarette and stared at the burning match for a long time. It had turned into a withered black stalk with a dying flame at the end by the time she lit the cigarette. She inhaled it all the way.

"And then he came. Oh God, you know as well as I that you should never do such things. Intercept a man and arrive uninvited. And I knew it then, and he knew it.

"His amazement was worse than his annoyance. The amazement was the worst. And nothing got better—I turned ice-cold all over, my lips and cheeks turned cold and then the rest of me, little by little. I couldn't say a word, nor could I answer when he asked me what I wanted. And when he saw what I looked like. . . .

"When he saw what my face looked like, he got scared. He probably thought I was pregnant and hurried to let us in the door. He pushed me in ahead of him and didn't say a word until we were inside and he'd securely locked the door. However painful it all was—well, in the middle of all the misery I was happy we were alone together. And it's quite possible that I deliberately stayed looking that way, to make him scared and to make him pay attention to me. You understand.

"I didn't make a scene, I didn't playact. But sometimes we do that anyway; perhaps we play out what's true about ourselves, but if pressed we could've hidden it too. Do you understand this?

"Well, well, no need to go into details. Because I stayed with him. I stayed the night. But my fear was lurking the whole time and I loved him the way you would, were it your last night to live. You understand?

"I chased my fear away that way. And captured him that way. Scared him a little too, maybe. But I captured a part of him that no one knew existed, the fact that he could be that way. His abyss—everybody has such an abyss, but not everybody discovers it."

She stared ahead for a long time. Then she said in quite a low tone of voice:

"This is where I should have started. Because this was the night I began to destroy him. This was the night we began to destroy each other."

○

It had become completely quiet around us, not a sound in the building. The street was asleep outside; it had stopped raining. Only the clock on the mantel was ticking, but I forgot to look at it.

"Up there where we live. It's different. Maybe it's the same other places too, but up at The Mine and in our town especially you have to be like everyone else. You can't hurt, not any worse than others. You can't have fun; you can't show you're having fun, at

37

any rate. Yes, it's worse than anything, showing you're happy. And above all you must never be different than you normally are; they can't take any surprises from anyone. Take, for example, a girl who never goes dancing, who isn't interested in kissing the boys. A girl who gets paler and more silent and ugly and hollow-eyed every day, a girl who goes to church and cries during the singing of psalms.

"She can't suddenly one day go to the youth center and start dancing, laughing, and taking a swig with the boys behind the barn the way the other girls do. There would be an earthquake at The Mine and down in town.

"I finally looked like death. And they'd become used to that, you see. I was only seventeen, but I was already regarded as a leftover at home. I was regarded as such and had to be that way and nothing else. I went to church because I loved organ music and because those tears were good to cry.

"They thought I was religious. But I sat there, seldom hearing a word of what our minister was saying because what he was saying did me no good. Maybe I'd hoped to find some of that solace which others find in this petty and powerful judge they call God. The one people accuse of wanting to avenge all those instincts he created in us. He who created love in one person but forgot to create it in another.

"No. No. Our minister wanted to construe the kind of love I had into a work of Satan.

"How could an all-powerful, just God allow Satan to create love in a young girl who had done nothing wrong? Can you tell me? Can you really tell me?

"Oh no. There wasn't much solace in what the minister had to say.

"He said being unchaste was the worst sin. He didn't talk much about the other sins people commit against one another. Gossip, pettiness, lying, the poison with which we kill one another—he didn't mention that.

"We kill unborn babies. Every day unborn babies are killed, but he didn't mention that. Who do you think kills them? I'll tell you!

"Ministers, among others. All those who keep alive the lie that Satan created our instincts and that lack of chastity suddenly turns into love when people get married. A minister reads a ritual and says amen over a down-payment of a few coins called a fee and then God has blessed the act. Yes, then it has become a duty. Duty, duty, duty, do you hear, above all; not pleasure.

"No, he gave me no solace, our minister.

"But the organ music gave me solace. And the altarpiece, the kind, kind altarpiece in our church. In its simplicity it gave me solace. The man who made it must have been a poet, even though he was no great painter. You know the scene where they take Christ off the cross. The figures are stiff and helpless and the colors all sky-blue and rust-red and yellow. But Christ, the dead Christ, the murdered Christ, his face is not peaceful the way so many have portrayed him. And his eyes are open! They're probably supposed to look glazed, but this painter has made them into a devastating accusation. Of the pulpit. The altarpiece is placed in such a way that the eyes look at the pulpit! And the pain, that burning, frozen pain—it *lives* in this murdered face! It lives there for all eternity, turned like a bitter accusation against the self-satisfied, judgmental cruelty of the one who is so proper as to be able to fit the crown of thorns around the heart of the one Satan gave in marriage to love!"

I wanted to stop her. I reached out my hand toward her to make her say no more. Her eyes were feverish and her voice eager in a way that made the words glow. She smoothed back her hair with both hands, undressing her face. Her voice had sort of collapsed when she started talking again.

"Oh, no. I'm not rebellious. I've never really said a thing. The one who receives the crown of thorns around the heart as the first bitter gift in life doesn't easily become rebellious."

She threw her hair back over her shoulders and stopped pulling it tight, and I put a cigarette in her restless fingers and lit a match. She didn't seem to notice, just sat there turning the cigarette around.

"A fantasy, a mood, is enough to make me feel happy. Well, what was I just saying? Well, it was the summer he went away, not saying goodbye or anything.

"It smelled of wild strawberries and you could feel the spicy smell of newly cut hay in your nose and your mouth and your ears and your skin. And everyone was happy about the nice summer. It was warm. But I, I went around cold.

"The boys and girls at The Mine went on bicycle trips, but they didn't invite me along because I wasn't the type the boys liked to bring along. I often wanted to go, thinking that if the boys liked me a little I would have fooled around and gotten in a good mood and maybe forgotten a few things. But they didn't even invite me. And I couldn't stand it.

"Then there was a dance at the youth center. Hello? I'll try to make this short. If only I knew what's important to include. It's important to me that you get the whole thing. Everything worth knowing.

"Well, I went to the dance one evening. Alone. Stood outside the door, along the wall, alone. The boys came over, fooled around, but they were drunk. They came out of the building in twos or threes and disappeared behind the trees, behind the rock outcroppings, behind the barn, and came back even drunker. Girls were looking for them at the door. They were nice girls; they just wanted to dance. They don't mind, girls in places like The Mine, as long as they get to dance. The other, the not so nice, only comes from wanting a bit of fun afterwards. Most often they don't want that. It just happens. And it just happens because it's wrong and sinful to dance in the first place, so it doesn't really matter if something else happens too. If young people out in the country were allowed, the way going to a fair and such is allowed, they would more easily make the distinction between what's just youthful fun and . . . the other. If the older people made a little fun for the younger ones, it wouldn't need to be like that. I'm certain it wouldn't need to be like that if they were helped out in making theater performances and such, helped by the older people.

"Well, I'm prattling a lot. What you should know is that I

closed my eyes firmly for a moment, swallowed my reluctance, and went inside.

"Later on in the evening the girls started going outside too. They sat on outdoor benches waiting for the boys, along with smoke and dust. They were pretty and young and had gotten dressed up for the boys and wanted to dance, but the boys just came in to dance once in a while. The girls danced with their coats on; there wasn't enough dancing to keep warm. And then they went outside too and were invited to have a drink, which they drank behind the barn, from the bottle, even though few girls like to drink. Yes. One thing leads to another.

"But that's the way girls get the way they get and become cheap. They just go along with the boys to get them back inside to dance again. Back inside they show off, fool around, mess around, and don't need to make themselves smile. They're having fun, they're happy. They think they're happy anyway.

"And I, I wanted to be happy too. Rather, I wanted to not hurt for a while; I wanted to take a little rest from hurting.

"I wasn't good at dancing. A little stiff and inhibited and critical. But there was a young sailor there. Handsome and nice, he wasn't particularly drunk, his breath just smelled a little, and he didn't mind my not being a good dancer. Maybe he felt sorry for me because I didn't even try to smile. He said nice things to me, about my hair and my eyes, and I should have been delighted because I wasn't pretty, but I just felt heavier and heavier.

"I should have left, had I only dared go back to my loneliness. The smoke, the accordion, the humming of voices—it was a bit quieting. And then this arm around me and the fact that he wasn't annoyed at my clumsy dancing—that was quieting. I smiled at him a little and then he said something about why was I so sad and tears came to my eyes and I thought it nice that he felt sorry for me and noticed my hurt. Can you imagine? Normally it would annoy me more than anything, someone noticing my pain.

"Nevertheless, I got even sadder. I got tired of dancing; my heart was so heavy, my feet got tired. But I didn't want to let go of this boy and become all alone again. That's why I just shrugged when someone came and invited him for a drink. They came over whispering something to him while he held me, waiting for the next dance, and he asked me to come along and I came along because I thought maybe the liquor would make me a little happy and dancing more fun. And then we walked up behind some juniper bushes and drank from the bottle. It burned, I coughed. But I wanted to, wanted to—I drank, stiff-eyed, and wanted to. And—hello? Listen here. Pay attention to this.

"I've always longed for beauty. Do you understand? I don't just mean to look at, nature and such. But . . . beauty. So, now you know what I mean and you will remember it. Remember it, all night.

"Happiness was supposed to be love of beauty and everything. And then, well, there I was standing behind the bushes at the youth center with some half-drunk boys, drinking liquor out of a bottle.

"Do you understand this? That had become my happiness for the moment. Yes, I turned warm, first my face, then the rest of me, and my thoughts got happy. And I danced more easily and hummed along with the accordion music. And this boy—his name was Eivind or Einar or something—his face had gotten red and his eyes warm and he looked at me the whole time and liked me and I liked that. But deep inside, oh.

"Deep inside reality sat, freezing. Way, way inside. And I sang more loudly and smiled more easily and let the boy hug me in order not to pay attention to all this inside me. I didn't let him kiss me, but I blew air at him and laughed and didn't get angry. He called me a little troll and I've always considered things like that stupid, but right then I liked it and I liked getting him a little light-headed, you know.

"But inside, oh God! Pain was waiting. And watching. And sending a message to my common sense. Which can be good. Every once in a while a wild grief would grab me, wild from accordion music and strange boys and my own laughter and from smoke and the smell of liquor and hot young people. Every once in a while it would grab me, wanting to choke me and paralyze me—well, that's the kind of happiness it was. That was the kind of happiness I would come to regret bitterly, but that came much later. Listen here.

"I'd laugh even more loudly then, you know. When *it* grabbed me and wanted to hold me tight again. And I would dance close to Einar or whatever his name was and I didn't turn away when his mouth searched out my temples and I returned his glance when his eyes grabbed me, and I felt hunted, so much so I almost lost my breath. It's the truth!

"Well. We walked toward home together. Just like the others, making sure we were by ourselves. Our arms around each other. And now I have to be quite honest: As long as we walked along the country road I wanted him to kiss me and caress me, generally. But I was afraid too and sang loudly so he wouldn't notice. But I wished it, yes. I wanted to forget everything and make believe that I was in love, that I was young and happy on a cool and beautiful summer night, like other young people.

"We met someone—well, I can tell about that later. But anyway, he asked, the way I'd expected, if we should walk into the forest a bit.

"And then suddenly I didn't really want to any more. But I just nodded and got cold at the same time and we walked along into the forest. It's a strange thing all that. I've experienced it often. As soon as we left the road I noticed that his clothes smelled strange and I didn't like his eyes any more, and I froze with fear inside. But I went along with him and pretended nothing was happening, thinking that I would let him kiss me and that I would kiss him back for as long as I still liked it. But no more. No more than that. He'd probably understand when I didn't want to any more.

"That's what I thought. And that it would be nice to have someone caress me and maybe be a little fond of me and understand that I wasn't happy and that it would all come to nothing— yes, that's how stupid I was!

"It didn't turn out that way. He became cruel. Probably with reason. But he didn't get me. We just fought. But, well, this is painful. So ugly. But you'll take this too.

"Such a beautiful night! Just imagine, the cranberries were just done blooming, it smelled so good, and slender young birches against a wide glowing sky clear as glass and little birds sleepily cooing in a tree, oh, no. You have no idea what it's like at The Mine.

"And then this. I told you, he didn't get me. I bit and scratched and fought back. I cried, thinking I'll kill him first—yes, I'll kill him first. But, well, during the fight . . . he finally let go of me."

She breathed audibly and whispered the words: "And then he didn't need me anymore."

It was quiet between us for a long time. I could feel my pulse against my shirt collar.

"Once home I couldn't stand my clothes. I hated them and they made me sick and I wanted to burn them in the stove. But I couldn't burn them, I didn't have any other clothes. I had to fix them, in secret, in the kitchen."

She put her hand on her forehead. I still don't know whether it was tears or a little smile that quivered at the corners of her mouth.

"And all my life I've loved all that was beautiful."

The living room had started to turn cold with a dead night-cold. She had tightened the coat around her body and pulled one leg up under her in the chair. It looked as if she were sleeping, she had closed her eyes. Her skin had a frosty look to it; her eyelids quivered a little. Her mouth was wrought into a beautiful arch, but it was quite without color. The clock ticked bleakly in the silence. I was looking at her and feeling the cold spreading from my wrists up through my arms. The cigarettes didn't taste good. When I got up, she asked without opening her eyes where I was

45

going. I said I wanted to get an electric heater. She didn't move and didn't answer.

When I came back with the heater, she was sitting with her head bent into her hands. I did not know if she was crying, and I felt poorly and unable to help her. I placed the heater so that it sent its warmth toward her. She removed her hands then and reached toward the warmth. She wasn't crying. Her eyes were dry and black. She continued her story from far inside her own world of thoughts.

"Well, I could sleep now. I don't hurt anywhere and could sleep if it weren't for the fact that everything has so strangely come alive for me today. You're not sleepy, are you? What are you thinking about? Dear. Your eyes look like they'll never close again. You can go nuts thinking about so many things; you must just listen to me.

"Listen here. This is just a small thing I happened to mention. You know I said we met someone in the road. No, no, this isn't disturbing or anything. Just something I happened to think of then or a short while later. Because they were singing, those political youngsters from The Mine. 'Those bastards,' he said. We didn't look at them when we passed. No, we never looked at them. But I thought about them, and what I thought about was their singing. Because it was real singing! And I caught myself envying them. I thought that none of them could be in pain. There are different kinds of singing, aren't there?

"It was the song of the invulnerable. Oh, what is it about this basic singing that they have? Can dry, inhuman *politics,* well, just listen to that rattling word—can it give young hearts warmth and make young eyes shine and give them *the song* in their singing, unless there's something more there. Well, unless their struggle is a struggle for humanity? Oh, I wish someone could have given me an answer to this earlier.

"Because now it's too late. Isn't it strange how most people know there's something terribly wrong with everything, but when it comes down to it they don't want any changes. Well, there were socialists there at home and they really wanted some changes to make things better and more just. But those who

46

wanted the changes executed and who actually did something to eliminate the very roots of injustice were hated like the plague. Those young people who organized to get our wishes and wants put into effect we didn't look at.

"But they sang. Yes, they sang, and that singing of theirs struck me and hid away in me and has sounded forth since, in glimpses. But now it's too late . . . for *me*.

"You know what a man once told me—no, my thoughts are leaping, but I want to tell what a man once told me. He said: 'Nothing grows by moonlight.' No, I'm getting quite desperate because I can't express what I want you to understand now—but we're too afraid to let this burning sunlight shine directly on us. We long for the sun, but we feel safest in moonlight. You probably don't understand this. No, but maybe you'll understand it when this night is over.

"Once I saw a girl, a whore, who was bending over to pick up some paper money. She didn't want the money; she said she wanted to throw it in the face of the man who had tossed it after her. But she put it in her purse in a terrible hurry—yes, I was looking at her hands. And I saw her eyes, the eyes of a provoked whore. She said the worst thing there is, that she was crap. But I saw her hands; they were so quick and so poor, and they put some dirty money in a purse because she couldn't afford to throw it in anybody's face and couldn't afford a little pride."

She rubbed her forehead with a desperate gesture and her eyes strayed helplessly. The hair at her temples was damp.

"No, where was I?

"This is difficult. No one can help me and this is difficult. Could I ask you to give me another glass of wine?

"Thank you. Things get clearer that way. I'll forget daily details that way and then I can tell you what I have to say before I leave.

"I was looking at her hands as she was picking up the money and it was then that I had one of those glimpses that could have turned to song in me. Yes, I felt that there is love in us for every-

47

one and that it resembles the love we waste on just one person. Did I say I loved that girl for a brief and dark red moment? I have no name for that glimpse, because it was a glimpse of love, a lightning quick pain of tenderness in me. But I hated that girl and everything that happened that night, and I was destroyed by a raw ache."

But you're probably bored now? The wine did me good. I'll tell you a little bit about my people at home.

"My sister was two years older than me. She worked in a cannery south of town, seven kilometers from home. She got on her bike at a quarter past six every morning, during the seasons. Outside of the seasons she helped mother in the house. She was the way a poor mine worker's daughter ought to be. But I, I had illusions of greatness. I liked school, I wanted to read, I would have kept studying if I'd had the opportunity. I read everything in the public library. Mother toiled herself gray, and I pretended not to notice. I had a girl friend who was a maid in one of the engineer's houses up there. She was stupid and I didn't like her, but I pretended to be her friend because there were all kinds of books in that house and I could go through the bookcases when the people weren't home.

"My father loved to read too, but he was always tired. He fell asleep over the newspaper; he fell asleep over books.

"My mother carried water. Her carrying heavy water buckets is about all I can remember. For twenty minutes she had to walk to fetch water. My sister gladly carried water when she was home. She was very good to mother, but I wasn't good. Not just because I was unwilling but because I carried a grudge. I was hating my mother because she carried these water buckets. Can you understand such things? I almost don't understand them myself. But everything in me would writhe when I thought about her with a grimy face, hollow-chested from carrying water. She washed the stairs and scrubbed the kitchen and she cooked and she never had enough money and complained that father used too much on tobacco. She did the laundry and had to

48

carry the clothes to the creek, summer and winter. I could have helped her. I didn't help her but I hated her because her life was so inconvenient.

"I felt a tenderness toward my father because he used too much money on tobacco and felt guilty about it. He was sick; they get sick up there at The Mine. They cough for a couple of years, get pale and stooped over, and they spit blood. You can see it on your way to the bus when there's snow in the winter. There are always tracks in the snow from those who are spitting blood. And the fatigue! Oh, what fatigue. And when you see those red spots in the snow downtown or around the country where the bus stops you know that someone got off there who works at The Mine."

She placed her fists against her eyes. I noticed that I was holding the armrests of my chair very hard, as if I was afraid of falling; then I relaxed.

"Mother and father were done with one another. She was done as a woman before she was forty. Not just because she was broken and not worth much, but they were bitter toward each other; I suppose it had to do with money. During the strikes that sometimes took place, it was awful. An evil silence stuck to the walls from all the bitter words that would not die after my father had slammed the door, left, and come back home, drunk.

"Words would fall, often. Words that could have been saved had father been able to smoke without guilt and had mother not had to carry water for half a kilometer. I think so, anyway. There was no other person involved; there's rarely any infidelity up at The Mine. And he didn't drink either, my father. Only when there was a strike or during a time when he was out of work. Then he'd get drunk sometimes and we had an awful time. But things were bitter nevertheless, hateful nevertheless. There was a quiet and restless hatred between those two people who had once been young and tender toward each other and who had once glowed for one another. No great drama, you mustn't think that. It was the insidious murder by everyday trivia.

"They kill each other slowly with malice and rancor. They are each other's prisoner. They become each other's sickness and fatigue and bitterness. They make children together and hate each other when children are produced.

"Oh yes. There were good moments too. There always are.

"I can't really tell what they consisted of, but we could feel it from the smell of the porch when we came home. Well, maybe I was the only one who felt it that way. For me it could belong to the way the cat stroked itself along the hem of my dress before I went inside or to mother's wooden shoes by the door, such things have a language of their own.

"It was a small yellow house that smelled of rats by the basement door. Sometimes it looked evil and at other times friendly. There were flowers in tin cans in the kitchen window, and they would sometimes wink contentedly at me as I approached the house.

"But most often there was a bad breath coming from that dirty yellow house, a cold breath of distress and complaint. And that's the way most of the houses were up there."

She was quiet for a long time. Once in a while a car rushed by outside. Afterwards it was twice as quiet. My small mantelpiece clock ticked on its shelf. The woman I'd brought home was sitting directly across from me with her hand over her forehead. Around her mouth there was a strange play of shadows that made it alive, even now that it was motionless. She slowly moved her hand away from her forehead and sat up a little straighter in her chair. She looked around my living room with a glance of displeasure.

"You don't understand this. You can't feel that kind of an atmosphere. Because you don't know the air in a place where you haven't lived yourself. You don't know the fear that hangs like a damp evening fog around the walls of such a house, the fear of tomorrow.

Well, well. I know it's useless telling you about all this. I don't know if you see what such a home does to those who grow up in it. There were only three of us children; I had a younger brother too. There should have been children. It should have been the way it was at the neighbor's, where children arrived who screamed and fought and almost starved and always had colds and were driven to the cemetery on a horsecart when they'd been run over by the trucks from the mine because there were too many of them for the mother to look after properly. But my mother couldn't do it, what with that heavy carrying of water. At any rate, I sometimes believe it's true that she purposely lifted things that were too heavy. Once I was at the window watching her lift a basin full of clothes that no man was even meant to lift. I watched her strain her lean body in a rage, and I watched her face . . ."

She stopped and caught her breath, there was a grating, underlying sound in her voice . . .

"And I hated her. I was just a girl then and I hated her because she forced me to drop my homework and everything and help her with the basin. And then I got there too late. She'd gotten the basin up and was squatting down pressing her hands to her stomach and groaning. Her face was yellow—no, I cannot describe that face. 'Oh Lord Jesus, oh Lord Jesus,' she said and I asked, 'Are you sick, mother,' but I hated her and didn't even understand it. And she wouldn't give in, you understand, she had to get the clothes into the boiler and finish her work. She told me to mind my own business. She was testy and nasty and said it would soon pass. And I don't remember any more than that, I just vaguely remember a few days later when she came home from the grocery store. She was crawling more than walking and there was a trail of blood behind her.

"It is such a long time ago and it happened a few times so that I can't keep the different times apart from one another. But I remember sheets full of blood and my mother's face on the pillow, distorted and nasty with pain. And those sheets! We put newspapers under her and burlap bags and everything, my sister and I, and she didn't want any outside help. She screamed when we wanted the parish nurse to come to the house.

"But that wasn't the worst of it. The worst was her lying there thanking God, yes, she was lying there in the worst kind of misery and pain a woman can end up in, mumbling prayers of thanks and being happy. She was happy!

"And my father? I've mentioned about his tobacco, how I would bleed inside when he bought a new box and sneaked it out of his pocket to have a smoke and felt guilty because he took a smoke—oh, that guilt! And the guilt when my mother was sick. Yes, he was the one I was fond of and the one I felt sorry for and would have fallen to my knees for. But I don't remember him other than as a shadow of guilt. I don't remember his face because what I remember and what stays in my eyes and my nose is blood, blood . . . and the whole house full of a metallic acrid and sick smell of blood."

She ran both hands over her face as if she was trying to brush away something. Her voice was tired and resigned.

"We had to wash the sheets in the tiny kitchen, my sister and I; we couldn't take them outside. My toes curl just thinking about it, even though I certainly have experienced worse since."

She became quiet for a moment and got up suddenly. She walked restlessly back and forth for a while, rubbing her knuckles against each other as though her fingers were freezing. "Oh yes," she said, "yes, yes Good Lord." I offered her a cigarette because it hurt to see her so nervous. The living room was thick with smoke and I asked if she had anything against our opening a window. As a response she walked over and opened the window and a fresh aromatic night coolness swept over us. She breathed in deeply and leaned on the sill and closed her eyes. She was turned half way toward me and she continued without opening her eyes.

"All this is meant to make you understand a few things. Because I wasn't very old when I began to harden myself against everything that bound me to all of that. Listen here, it's maybe a little comical, but don't laugh.

"Our outdoor toilet was located a short distance away from the house and I would sit there, preferably with the door open, and I could sit there and watch some bluebells outside that would jingle drily and quite slowly, and a small outcropping over which moisture trickled down, glistening in the sun; and then I would feel a limitless restfulness. And then the dream arrived. Not anything precise, just moving away from reality, just having life be something else, something that had a little of this restful feeling and that was without complaint and fear and trouble and guilt. Or I would listen to the rain whispering outside, in the shape of a gray wall, and this whisper and the delicate ribbons of water that fell and fell blunted my brain and made me feel only well-being, and that's why I later thought that was happiness. And freedom from fear.

"So I hid from reality, in magazines and books, and as the stories in the magazines were crushed in my hands, like empty shimmering shells, I found other things to read. About other countries and storybook journeys and about what human brains have invented and about achievements people have made. And inside me and from the pages of the worn books at the public library grew a new reality.

"Well, all of this made me cold toward my own people. I built a defense against compassion because I didn't want to help my mother but wanted to hide away and read. I didn't want to listen to her complaints about how expensive butter had become and how she had to toil and how insolent they were at the store when she couldn't pay all of the weekly bill. And I had to use the daylight hours for this reading of mine because at night you had to save on kerosene.

"Well, if I were to tell all about this, I'd never finish tonight nor tomorrow either. Just know this much, I was lonesome. I was lonesome among my own people and didn't belong among any others either. I couldn't stand my mother because she was humble in her discontent; she got happy when father received fifteen kroner from the factory during a New Year's celebration. She blessed the bosses because they gave the workers a gift and put up with her life as a slave and was happy about the most monstrous pains a woman can have because that was better than bringing more children into her misery. And I suffered for my father because he sinned with that expensive tobacco, and I ground my teeth and forced myself to *want* out of all that. I wanted to continue learning something and get away from the complaints and the wretchedness. And I wanted to hold my own book-learned reality in my hand and own it and would rather be mean and impossible than have anybody take it away from me.

"When I started high school I took the butter off my little brother's bread and mother didn't get the kind of kitchen curtains they had at the foreman's house, and I hardened myself and didn't want to think about it because father was with me. My father supported me and didn't want me to become an ordinary working girl. He said: 'Life has more to offer.'

"But guilt followed me. It gnawed and rasped and was always there. I finally felt aversion toward all of them because they wouldn't let my conscience alone. Well, that's the way it was. Because I didn't want, did not *want* to live their kind of lives and let go of everything I'd discovered life could offer people.

"Look at women like my mother. What do they know about everything that's created on earth, by nature, and by the abilities of people! She wanders joylessly between the store and the house; every once in a while there's a good gossip with a neighbor woman who's just as stupid as she is! Oh, but it's terrible! Where's the human in these humans gone? They don't even have the strength and the initiative to fight for their simplest of rights. To this day it's like that. They resign because they don't have the time to think about what they can do to get running water in the house and to get cheaper electricity. Nobody can take care of such things. The men have theirs, questions of pay and such in labor organizations. But their wives cannot get around to making life better for themselves. That's why I can't stand them. They become stupid and they become petty because their world does not reach beyond the store and the kitchen and the well. They become mean because they cannot stand the kind of happiness they themselves cannot participate in. They become malicious because they think someone else's accident elevates them a little from their own wretchedness.

"No! No! Ever since I was little I was one silent passive NO.

"But it was useless, you know. I was in the trap right from the start. I avoided my mother's prison and the other working men's wives' prison.

"These people, they have a door in their prison. It is closed but it's there. They can get up, they can gather themselves up, they can break open the door to their prison. The men have done that much. They had it bad earlier. And they don't have it good now. The men die nicely from silicosis and their wives die from toil or diseases of the uterus. But they escape death by hunger. They escape freezing to death. Now they're just killed quite slowly. First the joy in them is killed, then the human in them, and at last the body dies.

"But they have bread just about the whole time and they have heat in the stove. Yes, and they smoke tobacco and some have delusions of grandeur and send their children to high school . . .

"And I, I discovered too late that I'd ended up in prison. My own prison. And in my prison there is no door."

I had gotten up. I had to stretch a little and walk around. The words I wanted to speak were withheld for fear she wouldn't go on. She was quiet now. She was sitting in a rocking chair at the other end of the living room. There was a slow rush of rain in the streets outside. I closed the window and then it became quite silent in our home. "From my prison there is no door," she said slowly, taking a deep drag from her cigarette. I looked at her and wanted to say something once again, but I wanted to wait. I had

56

*to collect myself, and was standing there tapping a cigarette against the
back of my hand when she continued.*

"The beauty in life, have you noticed it? You cannot touch and
feel it. It cannot be grabbed and held. But you can suck some of it
in and experience it while it flees past you, so maybe some of it
stays, nevertheless. It's there in the feeling you have when you've
done good work. Real work, something that makes you efferves-
cent inside. It happens when you're strong enough to watch the
midsummer night's fire and rejoice in others dancing. How can
you explain things like that? I inherited a grand piano once. From
a man who killed himself. He had written to the town attorney
saying I should inherit everything he owned. He didn't own
anything but a grand piano. And when the debts were paid there
was nothing left of the grand piano either, the one I was to
inherit. And when I came to learn I was to have inherited it but
there was nothing left, I was ill, quite ill. I was in a clinic in
another town in the process of bleeding to death. But I got this
letter about a man I hadn't been to bed with and who wasn't a
relative. He had wanted to give me everything he owned before
he took his own life. This is beauty. What I lay there keeping to
myself then, is beauty.

"No. I'm terribly stupid and I can't quite find the right way to
express what I mean. But I told you, I've always longed for
beauty. But it's as if what I call beauty hasn't wanted anything to
do with me.

"That is my prison. I've never been able to get rid of things
hideous. Maybe I dragged the chains along with me when I tore
myself loose from my own people's prison . . ."

*She crushed her cigarette and got up. She turned on the radio and waited
for its light to glow. Shortwave telegrams began ticking out across the
living room at different frequencies as she turned the knob. Now and
again bits of dance music would flash up only to get quickly cut out.*

"We went away together," she said while she was busy with the radio.

"Well now, let me begin at the beginning. I don't quite know how it came to be, however; it's so long ago. But I think it was I who, I who, well, I who mentioned something about us traveling. An impulse I had. It happened on the pier; the boat was in the harbor. He was at the pier, just like everyone else, about a week before summer vacation was over. It smelled of gooseberries on the pier. There were boxes of gooseberries going to the city. And many people walking up and down the gangplank. Such a steamer carries with it a scent from all the places where it docks, a scent of country stores and burnt peat and sun-warmed rocks and cows and sweet grass. It lies there breathing and being busy. It has so many places to go. And he'd come home before the vacation was over, and I saw him on the pier and I was suddenly so confident and clever. I talked to him and I was bold and said, 'hello, how are you,' easy as pie. Just like a chance acquaintance. And then we talked the way everybody talks about the vacation and about the weather and about what a bore it was to stay in town and how nice it was to get away sometimes. I think I said something to the effect that it would be nice to be on board when the bell rang. Jokingly asked if we should go away, together. But my heart stood still and I changed color and didn't dare look at him, although I felt him looking at me. And I held my breath, not knowing whether he thought it was a joke or serious, but, well, the upshot was that we planned to go away. Willy-nilly down the fjords. Nobody would know about it."

She had turned the radio to a distant organ making swaying shortwave sounds out of a Strauss medley. She walked up and down the floor, dreamily staring out into space.

"He came to this city. Oh, we were so clever. We studied the schedules. We were to meet in such and such a place, at a ferry stop down the fjord."

58

She wiped her eyes with one finger and dried it on her coat before putting her hand back in her pocket. Her tone was unchanged, but her voice sounded as if she had caught a bit of a cold.

"I'll never forget this, you see. Not a single little thing. This trip of ours started as we studied the schedules. We were sitting at the cafe drinking ginger ale, and there were hardly any others there. I was happy, oh God, I was so happy. He had a pencil and a steamship schedule and he would travel by express steamer and then back again by another boat and so on and so forth. And I would take such and such a boat. Nobody would discover anything; nobody would know. We sat at the cafe with our wonderful secret, he was mine because we shared this secret. Well, then there was home; it wasn't particularly nice just then. My sister was expecting a baby and that boyfriend of hers was useless; he didn't feel like marrying her. Oh, there was a lot of discomfort at home during that time.

"And then there was the office. They didn't want to give me the time off. I'd had eight days off earlier and they didn't want to let me have a vacation, so I said I'd quit. It was sheer madness but I didn't care, you see. I would have set fire to the whole business just to have these days with my Johannes.

"His name was Johannes. I haven't told you that, but his name was Johannes. His name is Johannes."

She whispered into the air, "Johannes, Johannes, Johannes." A couple of fiery telegraphic signals shot through the organ music on the radio, cutting Strauss to shreds. I hurried to turn it down, and for a while we heard distant hooting signals through the hum of the glowing apparatus.

"Five days. No more than five days. Five days and five nights. But what an eternity of happiness. You're inclined to say that time goes quickly or that time's too short when you're happy. In retrospect these five days and nights seem like five weeks, five months. Because every hour, every minute, every second is burned into me.

"There was a little boardinghouse down in the fjord some-where, unknown and peaceful. Nobody was there but us. The owners were surly toward us. They understood that we weren't married; they understood it all. And we laughed at that. We fooled around and laughed at everything for no reason at all. We had a thousand little things to amuse us every hour, stupid jokes and impulses, wonderful meaningless moments that I have no intention of telling about, but they're nailed into my memory forever and ever. Because these moments gained their meaning from both of us being so extraordinarily happy. Yes, he too! I hadn't seen him like that, not before and not after.

"From the moment he stood there on the little pier waiting for me, oh, he shone. He was standing in a little circle of shimmering rain under the single light bulb on the pier, shining his smile at me. He had gone to the city the day before and had returned without going ashore at home. He had hidden on board and continued the trip and was waiting for me. And I arrived with my heart in my throat for fear he wouldn't be there, that he'd stayed in the city. My mouth was dry with fear and I was shivering with fear when the boat whistled before it came up to the little pier. And there he was. There was a shower just as they put out the gangplank and he was standing there in the rain on the pier, and to this day I don't know if there were other people on the pier or on board because all I saw was his eyes glittering through the shower, and there were just the two of us. But there had to be other people on the boat because it took an eternity before I could get ashore and I saw his eyes the whole time. Through an eternity of longing and impatience I saw his eyes and his worn coat and his hands were in his pockets and he was waiting and it was me he was waiting for and there were just the two of us. And first I gave him my hand and he smiled—oh, we were just a little shy because I was so happy and I don't under-stand how a human being can be so happy and not die from it all. And then all at once my suitcase was on the dock; it fell over on the dock and I felt only his mouth and his arms and his neck through my coat sleeve and streams of rain ran from his hat down into our mouths and we just let it rain and when we let go of each other there were suddenly some people on the dock gaping at us; they were probably scared out of their minds.

"There was no room for us there. We had to order a car and go quite a distance and it was expensive. I knew it was expensive for him and that he couldn't afford it, but I was happy about that, particularly about that. Do you understand? And what a trip. It cleared up. The moon was somewhere behind the mountains and the darkness was transparent as an amethyst. And we sat close together in the darkness in the car and were transluminated by each other. We didn't know if we'd find a place to stay where we were going either. It was like a fairy tale and wonderful not knowing anything, and he said that in that case we'd drive all night, we'd drive until we found a place to stay. And I closed my eyes and knew I could drive with him into eternity, even though we were impatient for each other and I was looking forward to having him. Longing was delicious; it was wonderful to know we were together in the car and were not going to be separated when saying good night."

The telegraphic messages had stopped. The radio was humming emptily and I turned the knob and found a tango on a French accordion. I heard her striking a match and turned around just as she sat down in a chair again. She leaned back, making herself comfortable, and looked as if she was at ease.

"It's strange," she said. "I'm not drunk any more, not even a bit tipsy. But I can tell you everything. I like telling someone now and I'm not afraid you'll be bored. This doesn't bore you, does it? You're tired, but you like my talking now, don't you?

"Listen here; there was a little boardinghouse—yes, there was room. We had to knock for a long time because it was the middle of the night and she had a nightcap on and was sour and angry, the proprietress, because we sat on the stairs kissing each other when she opened the door and I don't know if she really noticed. You see, we had to wait for such a long time between each time we knocked and then we had to kiss, you know. But we got a room, anyway.

61

"That was the first time we slept together. And that was when I learned something brand new to me, something I didn't know existed in the life of human beings: death's loneliness. He slept in my arms, we were entangled, but he slept and I was alone.

"Alone. Alone. An oppressive feeling of loneliness folded itself around me, and I hadn't known it existed. In the arms of the one you love you're more lonesome than if you were sitting on the moon, but I didn't know that then. Now I know it, know that you're never lonelier than when you love someone who's gone to sleep on you—well, it's just that way. And I was filled with a large sorrow and a large sense of the solemn. I put my mouth against his chin and felt that my mouth was cold. It was an overwhelming and beautiful experience. I didn't know what was going on inside me but I couldn't lie there quietly so I carefully disentangled myself and got up. I don't know if anyone would have understood what I'm trying to tell you, but it was an experience that overwhelmed me. Daylight was breaking outside and I sat with my elbow on the windowsill, smelling the bitter scent of potato tops rotting. Somewhere or other a river was humming. Otherwise it was dead silent. Oh God how silent, how lonely and silent. Just his quiet breathing. With the indifference of someone asleep. You love him, but he's in a different world, a world you don't know and where you have no business. I had to go for a walk.

"I immediately had to get out into the glasslike dawn, as if someone was dragging and forcing me out. I put on shoes and Johannes's coat over my nightgown and it was cold outside, morning cold after an August night soft with dusk, and all color was erased, like in dreams. The grass was gray and the mountains were gray with white veins of snow at the top; they were incandescent just like the white houses, and the fjord was silver gray and still.

"I walked across the field, making black tracks in the gray veil of dew. There was no sign of birds and I came out on the country road and past a little post office and the tobacco shop—its postcards and sheets of paper dolls and building blocks and snuff and tobacco in the window—asleep with its eyes open. All the houses were asleep with their eyes open and the gardens and the trees were dreaming in the gray light, and behind the post office the valley stretched its arms toward the mountains and the sky. They are mountains that look like they've been struck by sorcery and have been frozen while dancing wildly. They are mountains of courageous outlines and passionate rhythms, they are the most beautiful mountains here in the West. It is, by the way, the most beautiful place in Norway. The most beautiful in the world."

She made her mouth curve slightly; shadows of dreams were in her eyes. It was completely silent for a while. A forlorn intermission signal tinkled on the radio, a droll melancholy little tune.

"It is the most beautiful place in the world, that place where we lived on the fjord for five days and nights, Johannes and I. A little nook in the fjord squeezed between wild mountains that envelop the place in eternity and are frozen by sorcery and that stand there with their wild plasticity against the sky and can never smile and that are silent in all their thousands of years of wisdom."

In the apartment below a living-room clock struck two sad blows and I jumped a little. I hadn't heard it strike before.

"And I walked up toward the valley and could only hear my own shoes against the gravel in the road and the river that hummed. I couldn't see it, although it sounded closer now, but the forest stood there so mute, protecting it with its loneliness. And then a small ice-cold waft of air came off the mountains, enough to make the leaves on the trees start shaking and there were tears on their branches and the scent from the orchards was acrid and my hair touched my face just a little and the chill stroked my cheeks with a cool and friendly hand. I was sad and happy and full of ceremony and longed to go back to my friend, so I turned around and wanted to go back. But, you see, we still had a lot to say to one another, this morning and I. Because, as I started back, the tears on the trees had started winking and glittering and a pink tinge snuck around the mountains and dahlias and asters in the gardens had begun to smolder in the grayness; they glowed like jewels in the shadows.

"And birdlife? Half-grown roosters were having a practice session in all sorts of sounds. Dark and light and quite cheeky and helpless sounds, and a chicken cackled angrily for the loss of her sleep.

"You know, this wonderful place and I, we smiled at one another and Johannes wasn't part of it; he was somewhere outside this experience I wanted to share with him. And so I waded through the dew across the field, the deep green aftergrowth was bathed in a glittering veil of dew; it was a burning membrane of millions of diamonds hissing and sparkling with blue and gold and red and purple lightning, and I fractured them under my shoes. And never has the aftergrowth been so newborn and so infinitely green as it was in my tracks, and Johannes lived in my skin and my soul, but I was lonely and couldn't share my experience with him."

She was silent. The footsteps of late night wanderers could be heard on the sidewalk; they sounded metallic in the silence and some car or other haphazardly rushed by.

"I came back to Johannes. He had turned around and was curled up so that there was no room for me and I tried to make room and he woke up then and we made love but my loneliness was with me and I couldn't chase it out of my heart, although we were as close as two people can be, but we were in separate worlds.

"We went for a walk after breakfast. We were meandering up the valley, walking close together. I talked about little things at home and he talked about little things from his childhood, and he

64

drew a picture of those parts of Johannes who had grown up before I knew him, confidential little irrelevancies that fell into place and stayed with me. Oh, God, how such things can anchor a person to your soul with fine little threads you barely notice until the day you try to pull them up and discover that you're thoroughly intertwined and that they have a life of their own."

She leaned forward and was scratching the armrests.

"It's difficult to talk about this. My heart feels so heavy, even though it was one of the finest times I've experienced in my whole life. You have to help me, you have to listen to me and not judge Johannes, only I can do that. Because I'm sitting here, done with it. You don't know this, but I'm done for and I want to look back now. I want to take it out of its hiding places and look at it all. I have the courage to do that because I'm done for. No, look here, have another cigarette and listen to me.

"I came to know something today," she continued. "I'm really still quite numb. And I have to figure out everything that has contributed. I feel as if there is something to blame somewhere. You could say I'm to blame. But you're not always master of everything you do. You don't always do what you've wanted to do, and you don't have the freedom to act according to what you feel is right.

"Oh, God I'm so nervous now. How far did I get?

"You know, I once had five days and nights, five days and nights without shadows, where the shadows themselves were like beautiful marble reliefs of perfect joy. We lived far down the fjord, we were together, the man I loved and I. We lived in a long low shed of a room with horrible illustrations thumbtacked to the walls and packing crates covered with crepe de chine for cupboards and an ugly sink. But it was filled with our lovemaking, our breath, our whispering in the twilight, our kisses, and our laughter. Oh, what a palace of a shed.

"And you know that strange light that makes everything bigger and wider in late summer, yes, it spreads gold over those days between the mountains, rain or shine. You know that time when all the berries have been picked and all the houses smell of jam and just a few rank black currant stalks still hang there, hot and sweet to the taste. We hunted for those and found each other's hands and our kisses tasted secretive and dizzy in the dimness where sunripened berries and warm earth breathed. And we crept close to one another and I didn't feel any cold shadow of loneliness. I was insanely happy with him then.

"One evening we were out in a boat trying to fish. I can't remember if we caught anything; I don't think we caught anything. I just sat there looking at him, absorbing the evening mysteries and listening to the oars that slowly licked the water's surface and slowly made the oarlocks squeak. Then it got darker and a silver coin fell on the water's surface. There was a shower and the raindrops were silver coins that sprinkled down more and more densely. I got wet down my neck and the water boiled with rain and we had to hurry to shore and find shelter in a boatshed where it smelled of old burlap bags and the sea and seaweed and tar. And then it was completely dark. And when we went back to the boat day was breaking, a rooster crowed, and before we reached shore the little workshop had started humming, a hum we heard all day. I can still hear it and the hammering from the little boat-building yard. The mountain tops glowed with a sickly glow of morning sun as we went inside to go to sleep. We walked in silence and close together and found each other once more without words and afterwards we slept; we slept until dinner that day.

"Whenever we went on our little meaningless and happy walks he said how strange it was that we'd had to go to hell and back down the fjord to find each other, and I was happy. He said, 'I've come to love you these few days. You've turned everything upside down.' And I let his words sink way down into me and was happy. He said, 'I could have married you.' Yes, he said *could have*. But I was happy. A large and tender happiness.

"*Could have?* I could have been given the right to carry him on, to give birth to a new life made by him and me. I could have fulfilled what nature meant for us to do when it turns love into what the church and stupidity call sin.

"And a new kind of longing tightened around my loins and washed through me, a deeper longing than I had ever felt before, a tender and happy longing. It's meant to be, you know. Love that grows and lives in you is meant to become substantial and real inside you and make you fruitful."

The window panes glittered with thin raindrops that cried without a sound. Far out in the harbor a motorized ketch putted along, sounding very loud above the quiet city night.

"Well, well," she said into space. "Well, well. It's so long ago. It's a thousand years ago. It happened at the time when I was a human being, an alive human being, a woman with a purpose to be fulfilled.

"Well then. One day the trip was over. He left first. We were not to arrive by the same boat. He said, 'Yes, we'll meet again.' He kissed me and there was nothing wrong with those kisses. But I don't know what was wrong with me, I was filled with a wild despair. I thought about his saying we'd meet again and I recalled his voice that rejoiced and loved me, but fear and despair wouldn't leave me in peace. You know, it's terrible to think about, the unhappiness that sneaks into you with its cold shadow before you even hear its footsteps! Oh, that fear, that fear!

"No pain hurts more than fear that has no substance to it, that just chases you up the wall, being invisible. Don't look at me like that. I'm not afraid any longer. I have nothing more to be afraid of because today someone gave me what human beings are the most afraid of. It's visible in my heart and I can stand looking at it. But you mustn't look at me like that. Did I really scare you so?

"You'd better listen, I'll tell you the whole thing. Listen quietly and don't forget anything, don't forget.

"You know, animals have that kind of fear before a storm. We, some of us, experience it before something terrible happens.

"I had that fear back then; it ached like an abscess I couldn't see. I staggered around in the dark, knowing there was an abyss somewhere that I couldn't see. That little room. He wasn't there, he'd gone. I thought, I said it out loud, 'He's just gone home, I'll follow, he's waiting for me.' Nevertheless it was as if he was dead. No, not dead.

"Because death is not the worst thing that can separate two people.

"Oh, but then I remembered that he'd left his vest behind. He'd asked me to bring it in my suitcase because it was warm on the evening he left. And then I found the vest and I buried my face in it and felt that little intimate smell of a person who has made roots in all your thoughts. I took his vest to bed with me and I squeezed it in my arms. That way I could sleep.

"But I didn't eat during the two days I had to stay there alone—well, there was no boat until then. And when I was going back I paced the deck, whipped by fear. I told myself, 'At least I have his vest; it's in my suitcase among my clothes. He has to have it and then we'll see each other and then all will be well, all will be well.' When the boat whistled in the harbor at home I was senseless with a fear that you couldn't see anywhere.

"And when the boat docked . . . I began to shine inside. I was hot with joy, I turned silent with joy.

"Yes, he was at the dock. He was waiting for me at two in the morning on the dock. Our eyes found each other immediately and didn't let go. I handed him my suitcase over the railing before the boat was made quite fast and I jumped ashore before the gangplank had been put out and he took my arm without a word. We walked together and didn't pay attention to whether or not anyone saw us. We were walking, just the two of us, and the moonlight shone through the cloud cover and we went to his place."

A pale light fell across the rooftops and here and there a window watched the empty streets below with a lonely glow.

"I stayed there until morning. He said, 'I'll never let you go again.' Oh, tell me what that thing is we call happiness. Inside this terrible happiness there is a kernel of fear. A trembling sun-white cell that is made of fear. Happiness is what we think happiness is. For as long as he held me in his arms and kissed me and said he'd never let me go I was safe, safe. But when I was walking home, holding him in my heart, that little sun-white cell began to glow and twitch. I walked faster to get away from it. I ran and wanted to flee. I felt that small happy pain from him and the warmth of his skin and the words he'd spoken were a song inside of me. But I was being chased home by that tiny little fear that lives in all happiness and that makes it heavy to carry.

"At home unhappiness had taken up residence, for real. I squeezed my eyes shut and didn't want to see it, didn't want to see it. I wanted to be insensitive and couldn't afford to let anything slip in that could push aside my happiness. This rare and expensive thing, which was being happy for myself and being surrounded by love and beauty. I snuck around the bad feelings at home and wanted no part of it. I became awful and indifferent and snuck away to my rendezvous with Johannes. I desperately clutched these days with Johannes as if I knew one of us was about to die. I didn't have time, I couldn't afford to miss any of it. Meanwhile my father was getting more and more short of breath. He had a few attacks for lack of air and filled the house with fear. Evil words smoldered among the walls because my sister was expecting a baby. Her choked weeping stared at me at night in our room. The words that fell between my mother and my sister were a gaping abyss of hideousness.

"What my mother revealed about the ignorance of our class, the one that's forced on us, the one we're submerged in by force, was what makes so many of our women nothing but dirty bitches when the going gets rough. My mother's despair revealed the abhorrent leftovers of stupidity, the obscene backside of stupidity. The dumb maliciousness of someone who loses their head in helplessness and cannot pass the test.

"And my father was alone with the undeniable that came closer without disguise. He was the loneliest man death ever saw. *I* should have been able to understand him. I was *his* child. But I fled. I closed myself in with my own affairs and avariciously held on to my own happiness and didn't want to enter into the shadow of his death struggle. Because that silent struggle against the meanness of home, the struggle against that which grabbed his breathing and wanted to choke him, was a struggle against a graceless death.

"I told you. I betrayed my father during the most difficult time. I sought the intoxication I found with Johannes and didn't want to see anything else. Only once did I have any feelings for my people. That was the night when my sister was crying. I lay down in her bed to comfort her. But I already told you this, didn't I?

"I felt something living inside her, something living in her stomach. And later I felt so lonesome and, well, it was so strange because nothing lived inside me. I loved, I was happy, but my body was just my body without anything in it. But you know; I've told you this before and you mustn't get impatient. Well, I'll tell you how it went.

"It was during fall. A good time and a bad time. But I pushed the bad aside and made myself a stranger to it. My life was with Johannes. My life was those evenings when I snuck away to his place protected by darkness and rain and was expected by him and loved by him. But they noticed at home; they noticed that I stayed out nights and I was tired in the mornings and often late for the office and it got uncomfortable at the office and my mother got vulgar, the way mothers get with the best of intentions in mind. And I was cold and hateful at home and warm and happy when I walked in the darkness, knowing that Johannes was waiting in his cozy living room behind closed curtains.

"And then I didn't want it any more. One day I didn't want it any more. I already said I'd become awful at home. I defended myself by becoming coarse. I felt vulgar and disgusting about that and sick with willfulness. And I didn't want it any more.

"That was the first of November. I remember it because I'd gotten my pay, seventy-five kroner. I packed what little I owned, and I even stole a slip from my sister. It was such a pretty slip and I didn't have anything like that and she was just sad and expecting this baby and not paying attention to wearing anything pretty.

"I didn't say good-bye to anyone. But something caught in my throat as I traipsed away with my suitcase. Something caught in my throat as if I was about to lose my breath with crying, but no tears came and, I don't know, the whole thing was crazy. I've never been any adventuress. Seventy-five kroner and no more job. Because I didn't want to go to The Mine every day. I wanted to be down there in town where Johannes lived, and I thought something or other would materialize. A store or something.

"I found a room in a boardinghouse all the way down by the water. It was named Nilsen's Hotel and I regard it as a chapter, a strange and ugly chapter, this Nilsen's Hotel. You'll hear quite a bit about it."

"I hadn't said anything to Johannes about this either. All in all, we didn't talk much, Johannes and I. Sometimes he talked about the municipal government and such and a little about school and different things. But he never asked about my life. That was strange, but he never asked about anything. And it was always at night. We had to be quiet. Johannes was quite alert to anyone noticing anything. Yes, sometimes he was downright scared when he heard footsteps or something. 'Shhh!' he said. And he didn't breathe, he just listened.

"Anyway, everything I could have talked about was only sad and could have cast a shadow. And I was stingy about those hours with him. No, we didn't talk much.

"On the evening I checked into Nilsen's Hotel we didn't have a date. But I couldn't stand being so close to him and not seeing him. I could see a bit of the house where he lived from my window. I could see there was a light on. So I snuck down the well-known road, took the basement entrance the way I usually did, a little scared and happy, and scared again because I was arriving unannounced. As I stood in the kitchen my heart took to beating violently. It was dark in the kitchen. It smelled of paraffin and coffee, and there was a ribbon of light from the door to his living room. It was quiet in there. He could have been working, right? But there was something wrong with the silence in there. It was just as if a cold shower was running down my face and I wildly thought, 'He's working in there, of course he's alone and working.' Then a floor board squeaked where I was standing. It was an old house and the floor boards would suddenly squeak and I was shaking and hugging the wall and counting my heartbeats. Everything in my head was turning around. Someone moved in there. But some time passed, an eternity, a minute or so.

"Then he came. He came quickly through the door and he closed it firmly behind him. We stood in the dark. I held my breath. He didn't see me. Irritated, he said, 'Is someone here?' He must have heard my breathing. I couldn't master my breathing. It suddenly felt as if I'd been running violently and would burst. And I didn't answer. But he knew it was me, from my breathing. And then he came toward me without a word and pushed me along farther away from the living room.

"It was unbelievable. It was terrible. He wasn't glad I'd come. No, he was rather angry. I had never heard him like that. An evil whisper. What in the world was the meaning of my showing up like that, without his knowledge? What was the meaning of this?

"I couldn't answer him. I couldn't move, nor open my mouth. I wasn't thinking of anything specific, I just suddenly felt bitterly homeless.

"He glanced toward the living room door and he became a little kinder. Maybe he thought he'd been stupid to show his anger. He said, 'Why don't you come back down tomorrow night. There's a guy in there, a colleague . . .'

"Going back out, down the basement stairs felt shameful. Oh, God what misery. He watched my back. I felt his watching the misery I carried on my back as I left, leaving as quietly as I'd come. It was raining outside. It sizzled in the gravel and hummed in the trees and gossiped in the gutters and I heard the sea. Suddenly I heard the sea that I was not used to at The Mine and knew immediately that I would be hearing this sea constantly. 'Oh well,' I thought, 'then at least I have someone, at least I have someone I can talk to, at least I have the sea.' Oh, I didn't know all the terrible things I would be talking to it about, this only intimate friend I had for a long time."

●

"So he didn't know that I'd moved down into town. He said, 'Come down tomorrow.' That meant he thought I was walking six kilometers back in the dark of night and the rain, without even a caress. I didn't dare think about that. I didn't dare face the meaning of his just sending me home like that; that's where he thought I was going, right? And I didn't dare think about it, but the thoughts came anyway. He could have asked me to wait outside; the guy would have left or something. Well. I was back

75

in my room. It was a naked room with a draft coming from the ill-fitting windows and a kerosene lamp that smoked. It was cold and there wasn't anything to make heat with. My suitcase stood there, I hadn't unpacked it. Didn't feel like it, either. There was a bed, a completely strange bed and I didn't feel like going to sleep in it, even though I was unbelievably tired. It had a bedspread made of some kind of red satin and it had spots on it and looked unappetizing. Other than that, there was a very big chest of drawers with a mirror that reached to the ceiling and the mirror was broken. The washbasin was made of tin. It was rusty inside and couldn't possibly be cleaned properly. I could hear the sea the whole time, intruding as if it wanted something of me. And I was watching Johannes's window, feeling uneasy about what the sea wanted of me. It was just as if I was dreaming the whole thing. Home and all of that and what they must be thinking sort of didn't exist, just the way it is when you dream. What the sea wanted to tell me and what I didn't want to know seeped into me then. It was the fact that Johannes was lying to me. A nauseous unease told me. There was no colleague, or I would have heard voices.

"My teeth were chattering as I stood by the window watching the ribbons of light from Johannes's and the pulled curtains and behind . . .

"So I forced myself to think that they were working on something anyway and I was shaking throughout, nauseous from forcing my consciousness to accept that he wasn't lying and I shouldn't be suspicious and stupid. Then I remembered that he'd been angry and then I recalled this special atmosphere around him, a certain radiance, just like when I . . . when he and I . . . and then I shivered so hard I groaned out loud. I stood there until he turned out his light. By then the night ferry had come and gone. It was getting on toward morning.

"I went to bed with all my clothes on. I was so cold. I was listening to the sea threatening and threatening me down by the tideline. Fear and loneliness chased through me the whole time, keeping me wide awake. Once in a while I cried half-way out loud, without tears. I heard people in the building getting up, and

I couldn't go to sleep then either. But I was too exhausted by all those thoughts going around and around to manage to get up.

"Oh, God, it was a bad day and that has little importance because so much else happened. I'll be brief.

"The day after, well, in the evening like he'd said, you know, I went to his place with a shaky little hope that I'd been stupid and overwrought. I was so stiff and sleepless that a sort of shell formed out of my painful fear, keeping it quiet. But it didn't get any better, even though I told myself everything would be well as soon as I was with Johannes. It didn't turn out the way it should have because there was an accident waiting to happen inside of me. And he noticed that I wasn't in good shape, and he got in a bad mood which he tried to hide. That made the emptiness between us even larger. There was a cold abyss I couldn't help noticing and I wanted to throw myself at his feet and I wanted to say all the warm words that were gathered in me, but I was so frozen and helpless. And Johannes looked at the clock without even knowing it.

"He didn't say a word when I told him I'd moved away from home and was living close to him. He started looking through some periodicals on the desk. He hid away from me and fled from what I was saying. I didn't know his thoughts, but I felt they were not kind toward me. I didn't dare see what I had to see and I desperately thought, 'Tomorrow will be different, tomorrow all will be well again.' My brain was an icy lump. I didn't allow it to think. It was as if I was chasing common sense out through the roots of my hair until they burned. When I finally left him it was almost impossible to move my feet. They wanted to go back. I had to ask him something, talk things through with him. But I couldn't do it. A chill was keeping us apart and I knew I was on my way to an accident without being able to turn around.

"It's like having a nightmare. Your will is immaterial. You're running toward an abyss or you cannot move your feet. You cannot formulate the words that are burning inside you.

"We had made no date. I thought, 'He'll probably write a few words.' But he didn't write and every day I thought I'd go to him because I had to really talk things through for once and tell him that I loved him and get to know straight out . . . well, something had been missing the whole time anyway. I was feeling so bad I ended up staying in bed all day. I didn't have the strength to look for work. I waited and waited. A letter arrived that I tore open, thinking it was from him. It was from my mother. I've forgotten all of that because all I ever thought about at that time was Johannes, Johannes. But I think it was during those days that they told me my father was bedridden. He wanted to talk to me and I thought, 'Tomorrow.' You know, when despair has touched you, you can't escape, you're marked. Despair has picked you out and is holding you firmly and you find yourself in a whirling stream that pulls you around and around. Wherever you turn there's a large sorrow laughing and hatefully squeezing you. Well, father. Oh, father.

"Every day I expected Johannes to maybe show up or to send a message. Later I would go to see my father, yes, later, later.

"I walked from the bed to the window, from the window to the bed. And I'll never forget the smell in that room. An old smell of a thousand strangers; it was stuck to the walls and would never go away.

"The days passed like that, and the weeks. A new fear had arrived. My monthly business didn't come. Slowly a storm of panic gathered in me. And the money was diminishing and I'd been turned down a few places where I'd looked for work and I couldn't gather up any more courage right away. I had to postpone, postpone. Hardly ate anything. My thoughts consisted of two things only, Johannes and this thing in my stomach that had stopped. I was beating my fists slowly against the window, screaming without a sound that it had to, had to come and that Johannes had to help me, he couldn't really run out on me. And I knew despair would truly descend on me if I asked him to help.

"Well, a thousand things happened at once during that time and I don't remember their specific sequence, just the fact that there was a tumultuous stream of despair driving me up the walls without me dying from it, without being allowed to die from it.

"Then I couldn't stand it any more. I had to go to Johannes, had to talk to him. But when I stood in front of his door I couldn't do it. I couldn't write any letter; I wasn't any good at writing. Then I stopped him on the street. And I tried on a surprised smile, but my face felt dried out and frozen, my eyes strange and flat. He gave a flighty greeting and walked past. I wanted to call after him, but couldn't muster any sound.

"What was this? What had really happened? I ran after him, my throat burning. My legs wouldn't carry me. I called his name but no one but me could hear it; it was just a little gurgling in my throat. When I caught up with him, breathless and close to choking, he turned around, annoyed. 'It's over,' he said. 'I know everything about you now. It's over.'

"It's over. It's over. I was left standing in the middle of the road watching his back as he walked. And an icy wind blew and I was naked, that's the way it felt. There were currents running down my neck and a strange tightening in my throat. I had no control over it. Strange sounds came from my voice.

"I was standing there. And then he was gone."

She stopped to light a cigarette. A worried mother-of-pearl shimmer stood at the windows. A truck weighed heavily on the cobblestones outside.

"At Christmastime I went up to The Mine, without joy. The week before Christmas I'd gotten a temporary job in a tobacco shop. Christmas cards and Christmas tree decorations, a few toys and such; there was a Christmas rush. So I had some money. My sister had had her baby. I was worried. There was no snow.

80

The roads were white and frozen and clanging like stone under my shoes and pine needles lay pale and frozen under the trees along the road. The houses were hunched up around their coziness with smoke coming from the chimneys and I thought, 'I don't belong anywhere.'

"But I was looking forward to this just a little because I was bringing presents. I had brought a nice thing for my father, a little barrel with brass barrel hoops and lid, full of tobacco. And cigars and an orange. The others would just get oranges. I'd also brought a nice picture of Jesus for my brother. I'd bought it because a man was selling it on the street and he had only one arm. But I was thinking that I would make it nice for my father at any rate and have a good time with him.

"Well, as soon as I stood in the door I learned that my father had died a few hours earlier.

"I stayed in the door and my mother said I mustn't let out the heat. I stayed there with the door open anyway. Not a word, not a tear, not an exclamation. It was simply impossible to make my brain give me any orders to go inside and close the door. My mother was preparing food for the parish nurse, who was there helping to wash and fix up my father. My mother's hair was a mess and her face was flushed and she didn't spare me.

"She told me the price of wood. She screamed it at me, or that's the way it felt to me, anyway. Because I thought it should have been silent, quite silent. 'Well, there he is, I hope you're satisfied,' she said to me. 'Now you show up. He asked only for you and none of us others toward the end. He found no peace with death,' she said, 'because you cursed death for him and he wanted no part of the minister, so now he's cursed for eternity and it's your fault.'

"I don't know how it happened but there I was in the living room and he'd been fixed up, but his face wasn't peaceful and redeemed-looking. I thought, 'This is not my father. These dead hands and these white stockings sticking out from under the white sheet like wooden feet, this isn't my father.' His cheeks were completely hollow and they hadn't been able to completely close his mouth. There was a little crooked crack and the blood had not been properly washed away from the corners of his mouth, a black drop had congealed there. And I stood there with the barrel of tobacco under my arm and the two cigars and the orange in my hands, not knowing where to put them. I couldn't cry or say anything. I was like a mountain of ice with a storm of unhappiness raging inside, and most of all I thought about being certain I was pregnant. Nevertheless, it was as if one pain subdued the other because my thoughts of Johannes stopped aching for a while. There isn't room for more than a certain number of casualties in one person at any one time, which I realized as the thought stormed past me and I was grateful to be at peace with Johannes at any rate."

The radio started up with a continuous scraping sound and I hurried to turn it off. The silence was crashing afterwards. Somewhere or other a piece of machinery started up.

"The tears that wouldn't come to my rescue were raging inside me and I yelled inside that this wasn't my father. But the worn-out destitution that existed in all the shadows of his collapsed and frozen features, well, that was my own self. It seemed to me his dead eyes were burning under the lids. One of them wasn't properly closed and the blind whiteness was like a silent scream for help and no one could help him and no one could help me and I wanted to cry then, but my face felt like it was made of wood and no tears came. The parish nurse cried and said that the ways of the Lord were unfathomable and His grace limitless and I hated her. My brother put the Christmas star on my father's chest and then he went to a corner and cried and my mother began sniffling and talking at the same time with her lips pouting and from upstairs I could hear my sister sobbing. And I turned more and more dry and cold.

"But then I heard another sound from up there, a petulant and strange catlike child's scream, quick howls. And then my sister spoke comforting words and forgot to sob. There was something in her voice coming from up there that I hadn't heard before and I felt my face slowly getting warm. The child cried and he wasn't screaming with sorrow over my father but because he wanted food. I could feel my heart and that there was life in it and my mother wiped her face on her apron and asked if I wanted to come upstairs to have a look at our shame. In front of my father's poor, dead, worn-out face she said that—'our shame,' she said!

"But upstairs she talked nonsense to the little one who was sucking and sucking and who let out angry little grunts when he couldn't get a proper hold and she stroked his tiny damp neck with her work-worn index finger and then I really wanted to cry, but I didn't give in, oh no! On the other hand, I had to hurry downstairs and outside to throw up. Well, it was probably too much for me. I could neither faint nor cry, I had to throw up. That's when I thought, 'It's for certain.' But I thought, 'I've almost had nothing to eat, that's why I'm sick, and also all this,' but I knew I was lying to myself.

"There was a particular peace to the certainty too. A particular hateful peace.

"There was no one in the living room when I came back inside. I could hear the clock ticking, something we at other times never heard. There is nothing so dead and so quiet as a dead human being. The package I'd brought for him was on the chest of drawers, the tobacco and everything, together with some baby clothes. I heard someone whispering 'Father' and felt from the painful tightening in my throat that it was me whispering. I heard the voices of my brother and the parish sister coming from the kitchen, coming from another world. I wanted to fall to my knees in front of his bed, I wanted to kiss his dead hands, but I just stood there. There is nothing that can give expression to what you feel, such things only turn into playacting in comparison to what you feel.

"They had to come and get him the next day. The whole house smelled. By then he'd changed too and I didn't want to look at him any more. I was constantly throwing up. The parish sister said that his lungs had started disintegrating while he was alive. He had thrown them up bit by bit. I don't know if that's correct, but I do know that dying from silicosis is terrible and that they call it pneumonia on the death certificate."

◐

"My sister got married after Christmas. At first he was difficult
and didn't want to make support payments, but then he decided
he might as well get married. But you know, while everybody
was crying tears of joy because she was getting married and all
would be well, I was overcome by an anger I couldn't explain.
Well, while she was having a good time with her baby she became beautiful and her voice had a certain timbre to it, soft and
shiny. This thing about the child's father and marriage by force,

you understand, made me aware with every nerve-ending that nothing good would come of it. It couldn't possibly be what it was supposed to; there was something wrong with the whole marriage bit, I thought. At the same time I realized you couldn't have a child without it. But I'd begun to wonder why you couldn't. *Why* is it such a shame and misfortune? Oh, well, morality. Falling in love and craziness. But what's so morally right about a man being forced to go to bed with a girl he's no longer in love with? Well, what's the point in the whole act of lovemaking when it's been stripped of love and craziness and is almost being performed with aversion?

"Just imagine, that's morality. Something about all this was confusing to me. Not that I ever particularly liked Amund. But you know, I was on his side, you might say. During the child-support hearing my sister said she hated him, that she wouldn't touch him with a ten-foot pole and things like that. But once the talk came around to marriage she got happy and immediately willing. He left her a few years later. Everyone said he was a scoundrel. But I thought, 'What else can you expect?' The result of all coercion is simply to make you bitterly fight it. Worst of all is the money. In the end it is probably money that determines morality.

"The baby boy was contemplating his fingers and noticed with amazement that they moved. He wet himself and got annoyed at being wet. He was quite pleased to be changed. Oh God, I can't describe it. Nevertheless, it was a disaster, expecting a child of my own. Something inside me melted when I was allowed to change my sister's baby boy. There were hot little flashes of something resembling happiness. When he slept there was a warm odor from his blankets, an odor clean as dew. When I held him in the washbasin his eyes were stiff with happiness. He sucked his lips and held his fists against his chest and moved his legs in the warm water and enjoyed himself to the point of spitting with well-being.

"One day when I handed him over, clean and changed, to his mother to be fed, he smiled. Just a quick, mischievous look in his eyes and a crooked grin—his mouth almost lost its balance, but it was a smile. My sister and I quarreled in all seriousness about which one of us he'd smiled at, her or me. I really cried then, I cried a little, when no one agreed that the baby boy's first smile had been for me. Oh, but I'm prattling on.

"Can you comprehend why such a little fellow isn't always welcomed, by everyone, I mean? Why don't they greet his arrival with flowers and band music and a notification in the town square about a new human being having arrived in the world, complete with ten fingers and ten toes? Well, that the miracle has happened once again; that he should know we need him; that no one should forget to feed him so that he may grow, nor to clothe him so he won't be cold. Well, I really mean this. Because we don't even give them a crib. We betray them before they're conceived and nail them to the cross before they're born.

"Well, well. What's a woman to do? When she isn't married, I mean. Look, she can do what my sister did, what most women do, force the man to marry. Do you think many of these marriages are what they ought to be or good for the children? Well, I don't know. They probably stand each other and tolerate each other and some make the best of it, realizing two people can never become one, at least not by coercion. What if they didn't have to go through with it? What if a child was allowed to have a good life, to be welcomed into this world, without forcing anyone into anything and without becoming a shame or a disaster to anyone? And without becoming a threat to the daily bread or the roof over your head or the management of your life. Well, I think that the most insane thing that ever happens is our sentencing unborn children to a lack of life.

"Once again I've gotten away from what I wanted to say. I went to Johannes again, went straight in and knocked on his door one bright afternoon. It was like throwing yourself off a precipice in order to avoid being run over by a train. That's what it felt like when I'd gathered my courage and walked straight in. I wanted to talk about everything and I wanted to know what he'd found out about that was so terrible. I didn't know that I'd done anything wrong. I thought he'd love me again once he knew there had been a misunderstanding, and then I'd tell him about the other thing.

"Well, it was all about that time at the youth center. You know, I told you about my drinking a little and dancing and leaving with a boy named Eivind. And about what happened then. Gossip had seized the story and had distorted it in the time that had passed, the way gossip usually does. My being honored by such gossip, my being noticed rather than the other girls at The Mine, came about because I usually didn't take part in such affairs. I was the sorry sort who went to church and cried, which I was supposed to continue doing. It was quite incomprehensible the way that boy had presented the story when someone asked him. It was made to make them believe he had had me. He had fixed up the story to impress his friends and had dragged me through the filth as far down as possible, details and all, you know.

"This was what Johannes threw in my face. We were standing there; he hadn't asked me to sit down. I couldn't defend myself. I just whispered down into my coat collar that it wasn't true, but that felt like a lie because *something* was true. Johannes probably didn't notice anything besides my trying to lie my way out of something, and he smiled. Just imagine, he smiled, an evil smile. He wasn't jealous and angry and sorry, just full of contempt. And he took the opportunity to tell me that he'd known the whole time what kind of a person I was because I'd been willing from the very first time, in the forest, you know, that very first time. And then I couldn't answer with a single word because my throat was full of tears that wouldn't flow. A thousand things stormed through me that I wanted to tell him but not one word came out. Oh, he would have understood . . .

"Well, we made love; it couldn't happen otherwise. But there was something separating us even further. The fact that he even wanted to touch me, still believing all that stuff. It was out of despair that I got as crazy as I did and loved him the way I did. It was out of rage over everything I couldn't say in words. Out of fear and desperation I loved him, was new to him and made him new. I was with a stranger, one who liked me and experienced me and had a good time that way, but who didn't love me one iota. And even though I was thoroughly unhappy and lonely when I left him, I had a tender little happiness to clutch at; despite it all he'd taken me in his arms and received me.

"Well, that's how poor I'd become."

More and more often you could hear footsteps on the sidewalks outside. A streetcar screeched in its tracks at the tram depot some distance away. A sluggish gray light was pushing against the window panes.

"Back in my rented room fear took an icy hold of me, like never before. There was a shimmering aurora borealis that night and I didn't light the lamp. I stood by the window with my coat on, freezing and thinking . . . 'Won't it come, won't it come?' . . . It had been almost three months and sometimes I'd thought it would maybe come. I didn't have any more money. Mrs. Nilsen, who owned the hotel, said I could live there for free if I cleaned all the rooms and helped out with the guests. I remember that aurora borealis like it was something emanating from me, as if my own fear was drawing a picture on a cold, bottle-green, starry sky. The sea was quiet. There was a brittle murmur and tingling at the tideline, and an ingratiating whisper inviting me to come ahead, to come to the only place left to go.

"During the day I made other people's beds and emptied chamberpots and sometimes I threw up and would cry with loneliness. When nausea overwhelms you, you feel the relentless pain of nobody caring. But, you know, there was something, right in the middle of it all . . . I ate, well, we all do that, but I was in a period of such sadness and grief that normally turns all food to sawdust in my mouth. That's why I have to tell you this. There was a gnawing hunger and I was given three slices of bread and a cup of coffee for breakfast. There was just syrup on one slice and only bad-tasting margarine on the others. I was only thinking about the bread I was eating and that became such a big impor- tant event in my life that I forgot everything else. It got me out of bed in the morning. I looked forward to that food and I was angry that there wasn't more of it and I didn't think about anything else then. But I poured the coffee down the drain when she wasn't looking and I would steal milk whenever I had the opportunity. She bought milk for her cat and the half-grown boy and she guarded that milk. Whenever she thought the milk in the pitcher had diminished, I'd say I'd given some to the cat. Sometimes I would drink it all because I couldn't stop. I was given dinner in return for doing the dishes, if there were leftovers. Normally, I was picky. I didn't like eating the leftovers that came back from the table and that other people had dug around in, with congealed gravy and lukewarm potatoes. But I ate them greedily and I stole cold potatoes and I stole bread in the evening after she was in bed because there was no evening meal provided for in our agreement.

"Well, in just a few weeks my life had become such that everything was irrelevant compared to lying in wait for the building to quiet down so I could sneak down in silent panic to snatch bread and cold potatoes, which I feverishly devoured.

"Well, you know, that was what drove me to overcome humiliation and rejection and my debilitating shyness and made me look for a job that could provide big bags of rolls, delicate wheat rolls. You know, I would have bought truckloads of such rolls had I just been able to make some money.

"I got a temporary afternoon job in a tobacco shop. And fear was making me cold and despair quivered somewhere inside me, but I bought milk and rolls until I was tired of rolls and then I bought strange expensive things to put on my bread, thinking I couldn't live without them. At those moments when I held the glass of milk to my mouth and felt the mild coldness of milk running down my throat and quieting my whole body, I was happy. Maybe it sounds strange because there is nothing noteworthy or dramatic about it, but at those moments I was perfectly happy. The nausea went away too. I didn't throw up when I had decent food and something I liked; besides, I liked everything. You see, there were many good moments.

"You must listen to this because I've thought such a lot about it. I was used to being upset and at odds with myself, and now I had all the reason in the world to be. Then to find there was room for good moments, for well-being; I no longer thought badly of Johannes either. I did long for him; he was like a bleeding wound inside me. But the fact that he didn't care for me no longer caused such an ache and I fell asleep at night with a satisfying fatigue and I cried only if I would wake up later and have to think about things."

Cars were hurrying along outside on the asphalt, leaving an expectant silence in the streets. Then a solitary horse and wagon clattered along. There was a sonorous rattle of milk pails.

"When you wake up in the night, not needing to go back to sleep right away and not having anything else to do, you have to think and your thoughts arrive by rank and file. All the thoughts you don't want to notice in the daytime. The thoughts that came to me . . . oh, well.

"Seventeen kroner a week and free room and breakfast. As long as it was just me at any rate, without a child. And what might happen with a child? Chased out of the house, quite certainly. Forcing Johannes to pay child support. Forcing my Johannes.

"Arnhild, a girl up at The Mine, got twenty-five kroner a month. She wanted to be brave and keep the child, she did. But her parents didn't want to be associated with such disgrace, so she had to leave. Nobody wanted her in their house with a crying child and, besides, nobody wanted to take in the kind of girl who took up with men and got pregnant. When you have children of your own you never know what kind of contamination such a child might bring to a home; well, you've heard such talk. She could either work at The Mine or do the wash for people, but she had to have a place to live and someone had to look after the child in the daytime, one thing after the other. She was taken in by an old tinker who soldered pots and riveted pans. His was an old shack and he drank for a week out of every month and was the laughingstock of all the children at The Mine. Otherwise, he was a nice enough man. He was a tinker who had settled down and he was kind enough to marry Arnhild. But every time he got

90

drunk he would torture the little boy and in the end Arnhild had to give him up for adoption. Apparently, he was placed with good people. But Arnhild could find no peace and she did not love the man—how could she—and there was nothing but poverty because he drank and people didn't always need things fixed and maybe weren't always good about paying for it either. I don't know how it all came out, but she looked terrible after a while and I often thought that I would never be so stupid about things.

"This and lots of other things came to me as I was thinking during the nights. Because I would like to keep my child too and have it in peace. But what kind of peace? Mrs. Nilsen told the story about a girl who worked for some well-to-do people she knew, and when the girl got pregnant and that was discovered she was fired. I could tell from listening to Mrs. Nilsen how people acted in such cases because she was quite kind and what you'd call a good person, but she agreed that such girls should be fired. She also agreed that the seamstress, Borgny, who made men's trousers for two kroner a pair and who also had a child, was right to keep her child indoors all year long and never let him out because you couldn't go around town displaying your disgrace. As soon as Borgny's Nils went to school, it turned out that Mrs. Nilsen had been right. I didn't know that until later. He was still little then and I thought it made no sense to keep him inside and not allow him out to play with other children.

"It's strange that I should be mentioning him now, by the way. Not many days ago I read in a local paper from home that he was under suspicion of burglary and had been placed in custody. But, damn, I got away from what I was talking about. Where was I? Yes. No, I was reminded of the day Mrs. Nilsen told the story about that girl.

"We were sitting at the kitchen table eating breakfast. I was listening to her and tearing my slice of bread into little pieces, putting them in my mouth. I felt my stomach become a burden. Well, it was as if it grew and got heavy while I listened to her. The cold and clammy fact came creeping over me that I couldn't just let time go by, drinking good sweet milk, seeing my arms get

91

rounder, forgetting how desperate everything was. Among all the thoughts that came tumbling down on me at night, this was the one that weighed the heaviest: Mrs. Nilsen, who slurped her coffee from the saucer, straining it between her two upper teeth spaced on either side of her mouth, who was kind and nice otherwise but who found it just that someone in such straits as I should be thrown out into misery with no place on earth to live. There was heat from the stove and a smell of dry firewood and coffee and warm soapy water in the kitchen. It was so nice and cozy that it made me feel cold right then. Outside, snow was falling thicker and thicker, coming to rest on the roof of the woodshed. A few sparrows were sitting on the clothesline, fluffing themselves up, being uncomfortable and discussing the dubious situation.

"I was staring out the window. Naturally, that way she couldn't look straight into my face, you know, and I would chew these pieces of bread whenever I remembered that I had bread in my mouth. My hands were so clumsy whenever I went to break off a piece of bread. I remember this because I relived it in detail at night and I would cry some then.

"Well, it got worse and worse, you know. It was as if I was two people. One who would just as soon be happy and carefree and one who looked down a gaping abyss where the future was concerned. And the abyss came closer every day, you understand. I couldn't let time pass without doing something.

"Well, I pulled myself together and went to see Johannes because I thought he could give me some advice. There was really a warm little current of hope in me because I thought he would be good to me when he discovered the kind of difficulty I was in. Well, I'll never forget that day. I had to gather my courage. I went for a walk. It was even a Sunday. It had snowed quite a bit, and when I turned around to go back to town it had suddenly stopped snowing. Suddenly. The sky was black with snow, but the world was as white and transparent as the frailest porcelain. The trees and bushes and the fence along the road were a dreamscape ready to burst at any moment, right in front of my eyes. A feeling that all was unreal came over me. I was dreading the situation and didn't know how on earth I'd be able to say anything. I didn't know what to say and I was trying out different ways of saying it.

"'Johannes,' I wanted to say, 'I'm pregnant.' Or, 'Johannes, listen, I have something to tell you.'

"Then, all at once, I felt a terrible fear and I looked around, not knowing what it was. The sky had turned blue without my noticing it. The sun was shining on all that new snow, swelling as lightly as foam all around. The world was suddenly a sparkling white and golden fairy tale, just the way something can suddenly spring to life in your mind while you were walking around dreaming. I've never seen the fjord so blue as it had become that day. All this overwhelming blueness hit me like a pain in my chest. Yes, you may well look at me. It was just that all of a sudden I was standing in front of the building where he lived and I didn't know I'd come that far. I was not prepared for the fact that now, right now at this moment, reality was about to happen.

"'Johannes, I'm pregnant.' No, not a word came. Just as though my voice and my mouth were incapable of comprehending this message from my brain. Johannes had just lit a fire in the stove. The flame was flickering and growling in the kindling and there was a faint smell of burnt paper. The roar in the stove made the room even colder. Johannes had just come inside with an armload of wood. I can still feel how startled I was when he dropped it on the floor. He brushed off his hands and looked at me with surprise. I was standing there in his living room, my hair wet from the melting snow and my coat all wet. There was a little puddle on the floor from my boots.

"Maybe there was a displeased look in his eyes at first. But it vanished and he kept standing there with his hands held together, forgetting that he was done brushing the dirt off them. He kept standing like that while his eyes slowly lit up. Have I ever told you what kind of eyes Johannes has? They're the kind that sparkle with kindness. We stood there for a long moment looking at one another, until my face got hot. Warmth flowed through me from the way he was looking at me. He was the one who did the talking. I can't remember everything he said; it wasn't anything much, but I remember that he thought I was pretty and was surprised at how pretty I was. He'd never seen me look so pretty. And I was so happy that he thought I looked pretty that I couldn't say a word. I let him take off my coat, thinking that now I had to say it, now I'll say it. But I said nothing. Nor did I say anything while he unlaced my boots. Everything I couldn't say made my body miserably wild when he pulled me toward him.

"Afterwards he smoked and was busy with his own thoughts and didn't notice that I was crying quietly. Then he started talking without looking at me and his words made my tears disappear. Every word landed in my whole body and paralyzed it so that I was completely quiet, listening to him. Well, there was something he had to tell me, which was that I must be reasonable and considerate. We were good friends, right? But nothing more. And I couldn't just show up like that, it could be inconvenient. He had become worried that I would come without notice; it made him nervous, but he would write a little note when it was convenient and we would have a good time together just like before, but only when it was convenient. He had a lot to do, he was tired from working at school and . . . well, along those lines. I can't remember it all. He mentioned the other thing, you know, up at The Mine. He was not angry and it was none of his business if I wanted to have a good time. But it was a small place and I had a bad reputation. I had to understand that he was a high school teacher and so on.

"I managed to get into my clothes after a while. He was talking the whole time and didn't look at me. The sparrows were chattering irritably outside in the snow. Then I noticed that they stopped and it got very quiet. When I looked out, it was snowing again. Snow was falling from a blue sky. Quite silently the snow was sifting down and the sun was completely red and dropping heavily down across the buildings in the west. The living room had become warm and twilight had fallen while the sun still shone. And a terrible crying spell came over me. I was ready to leave when I was completely knocked down by crying I couldn't control. Well, Johannes was surprised and a little irritated. He could not imagine my taking it so badly. He thought it unreasonable of me, too, because he had given me no reason to take our relationship so seriously, he said. He thought we could have a good time together without getting hysterical.

"I thought I was falling apart completely and could not for the life of me stop crying. It had gotten completely dark. We could see the red glow from the stove vent and outside it was blue with snow the sun had abandoned. But he wanted to comfort me, you know. He held me and stroked my shoulders and said we would go away from the town again. We would go away from town because there was so much gossip, and everything would be different when we got away for a while if only I'd be reasonable and not take it seriously. Well, well. I stopped crying after a while and he gave me my mittens. He embraced me when I was about to leave and kissed my face. I shouldn't cry, young and pretty as I was, and I should go home now and take it easy and not think silly thoughts that made things difficult for him and me both. But I stayed on. I wanted to leave, but I stayed on. I noticed that he wanted me to leave, but I stayed on. He looked at me. He must have sensed something. He asked if there was something special. And I stayed on and couldn't say anything. He held my arm and wanted to show me to the door. He was talking in a kind way as if he was afraid of something.

"I moved his hand away from my arm then and said it.

" 'I'm pregnant,' I said.

"None of what I'd planned to say came out, just that.

"I couldn't tell you in sequence all that happened then. He said I was lying. He said I'd invented it to trap him, but I wouldn't succeed. He called me ugly names, words I cannot mention. He was beside himself. If I wanted to extort money from him, I was welcome to fleece him, he didn't have much. I kept on standing in one spot. I remember I was very calm inside. An evil calm. One minute he asked me to pack up and leave, the next he asked me to sit down so that we could talk calmly about this. I stood still. He said I wanted to ruin him. If it was marriage I wanted, he'd have me know he couldn't marry just anyone. Well, he was quite desperate and I couldn't help feeling sorry for him. Suddenly he was the desperate one, he was the helpless one, he was the one asking what in the name of heaven we were going to do now. I almost had to smile. I felt older than him. But I don't think I smiled. I just heard my own voice, which asked him if there was someone else. He got angry and said, 'What nonsense.' Then he walked back and forth a bit, then looked at me and said there was no other woman.

"I sat down then and he asked me questions as though interrogating me about whether or not it was true and not just something I was making up. And I answered yes, quite loudly. But when he asked if I was sure it was *him,* I didn't answer. So he went into a spell of anger and cursing, but he finally pulled himself together. He lit the lamp and sat down. After we had talked for a long time it was decided that I should go to a doctor and get him to take it away. He put some paper money in my hand. I looked at it with disgust.

"He must have been disturbed. I didn't say anything when he took my boots off once again. He was wild and incredible.

"Quite a long time later I was standing outside the building, ready to go home. The stars were out and the sky shone from the northern lights somewhere behind the hills. Snow, silence, and a delicate, snapping frost. And the snow lay green as glass everywhere. I was tired and hungry and felt misused in every way. Inside my mitten there was ugly, ugly money burning my hand."

○

"I wonder if any man can understand what a woman feels while in such a doctor's office, the first time she sits in the waiting room with that particular errand. There she sits, a double offender, quite alone. Yes, a double offender. She has sinned, that's number one. And then she wants the doctor to help her commit another offense. It *is really* an offense. You've seen pictures and illustrations of those little fetuses, of a touching and marvelous development, of life being created cell by cell, all of which change from day to day, from hour to hour, according to the laws of nature.

Something is greedily absorbing nourishment, something that has already, from the very first moment, been given its talents and abilities from an unknown number of ancestors, yes, a surprise package full of talents that is human life eternal. And this must be killed. This piece of eternal life is killed every day. Oh, yes, yes, they may very well forbid us to remove it, in the name of morality and the Bible. At the same time they force us to remove it in the name of morality and the Bible.

"There was a seamstress in our town, seamstress Borgny. She didn't let herself be forced to remove it. She kept her child and didn't become amoral as a result. She just worked herself to death to keep him. And how did she keep him? She couldn't show herself in his company. He turned into a swamp plant and has been sickly ever since. All these talents that can be developed when allowed to grow right, what happens to them? What happens to them when such a little twig of a boy is brought together with other children and is daily reminded that he's of a different and worse kind than the others: of an utterly disgraceful kind? Oh, God, I get furious. When things go wrong for such as him, and they probably do because you cannot escape such a greeting into this world unscathed, well, then The Righteous Ones wisely shake their heads and say, 'What did you expect with a mother like that?' Have you ever heard that one? May every person who ever said anything like that have their tongue cut out and cut out again should it grow back!

"Well, you end up doing what Borgny did, or a girl like Arnhild, who had to accept a marriage to an old drunken tinker to escape disgrace and poverty. If she's a maid she risks being fired. If she works in a factory she has to be off work because there is no one to properly care for little children. So women prefer to have it removed, and there are so many women who have to get rid of it you wouldn't believe it."

She breathed out as though she'd been running. Her eyes were burning black. Distractedly, she reached for a cigarette, put it back, reached for it again. I went to light it for her but she continued talking and didn't notice. The match went out.

"Well, the doctor really isn't allowed to do it. All life must be protected. Isn't that what they say? Even so, new little beings are brought into this world, which does not want them anyway. That's the way it is. I've thought and thought about this, until I've thought I'd go crazy. We crucify completely defenseless little lives that haven't had the time to do anything wrong because they're in the way. In every way, they're in the way. If we're discovered doing it, we're punished. Yes, with disgrace and infamy. And if they're not murdered while still in the womb, both they and their mothers are crucified, slowly. All through their lives. This is what women don't dare do, no, by God. It's what I didn't dare, being thrown out for life with a child entitled to no other human rights than mother's milk.

"So I did it. But not until later. Listen here; first I was given some pills and things and was told to scald my feet in hot water and jump and run and lift heavy things. The pills gave me gastritis and ringing ears. Lifting? Well, I went down and lifted the neighbor's boat. It was frozen solid and had a tarpaulin over it, covered with snow. This was at night. If someone had seen me, they would have thought I'd lost my mind. I can't help laughing 'cause I got a nosebleed and tore my back so that I could hardly move for a few days. And then I ate, well you should have seen how much I ate. Cooked up quarts of oatmeal soup because I'd developed such a passion for eating it often. My body demanded food! And I ran up into the mountains, ran until my heart barked in my ears and whistled like a flute in my nose and throat. I ran until I collapsed, literally. What if someone had seen me? Well, it was ridiculous. And I'm here to tell you that thousands of women are running, jumping, struggling, abusing themselves, and being ridiculous. Within their hearts they turn into buffoons and perform ridiculous acts, which goes to contradict the notion that they don't want children because it's uncomfortable. And it's deadly serious.

"There was moonlight one evening and I was closing up Mrs. Nilsen's chicken house. I climbed up on the chicken house roof and looked around, like a burglar. No one was in sight. This is so funny it could make you cry. Not far away, on a rock outcropping, Mrs. Nilsen's hugely pregnant cat was licking its paws and looking at me with some interest. The cat made me feel ashamed—yes, can you imagine, I felt low as a dog because of that cat sitting there, fat and satisfied with a bellyfull of babies, finding its world in good order and viewing my behavior with skeptical curiosity. Oh, this is really funny. I stuck my tongue out at the cat, but it didn't give a damn. I called it a fresh tart. At that, it barely moved its head and found me completely nuts. It sat there with one paw lifted, nearly forgetting to bring in its tongue—oh, it was so cute I had to cry a little because in just a moment I was going to throw myself off a six-foot precipice. A cat can do that kind of thing for pleasure and to exercise its power, but it is a civilized being and just wouldn't do that when it's pregnant.

"Well, I jumped. I clenched my fists and called upon God and the devil and jumped. There I lay, convinced that I'd smashed every bone in my body.

"Then there was a scream, a bellowing as though from someone driven to panic by the sight of ghosts. I was lying there crying because it was the only thing I was capable of for a while. The scream had not come from my throat. No, it had come from Mrs. Nilsen. She'd come from the outdoor toilet at the moment I jumped. She'd seen me in the air, my hair and skirts flying in the moonlight. You may well smile. She thought a witch had come out of the sky. She thought it was doomsday, she did. The cat had run away. A cat most definitely wants no part of anything that crazy. Later, infinitely later, when she'd fetched Gunnar, her son that is, and they'd lit the kerosene lamp and were advancing in tentative procession to see what this could be all about—then she ended up having to sit right down, laughing, and rubbing her arthritic thighs. I'd given some kind of an explanation for my behavior, but I can't for the life of me remember what I invented. I just remember her groaning, 'Oh, youth, oh what youth can dream up these days!'

"And I wasn't the least bit hurt, but she had to help me inside, she and her son. When they looked at me in the kitchen light she was quite shocked. I don't know what I looked like, I was afraid of the mirror. But I was shaking so hard I could hardly stand up. She got me into bed and gave me warm beer with cloves and tucked wool blankets around me and told me to sweat. Mrs. Nilsen was among those who believed that all the ills of the world could be driven away by sweating. It felt good to be taken care of that way, and I cried as though beaten because she was so nice.

"But I was lying there thinking it had to come. I lay there thinking that nice ladies almost don't dare step across a doorsill for fear of losing it and I'd done more than almost anyone could stand. Nevertheless, my stomach felt as if it was full of cotton. Completely deaf and blind to all my frantic efforts. During the night I had to go downstairs to eat. Eat, mind you!

"The next day I was healthy as a horse and hungry as could be and had a bloodshot eye.

"I stopped all that idiotic self-torture. It was to no avail, anyway. By then I'd learned to recognize the character of what was meant to become a human being in my stomach. It had a personality, a tyrant who didn't give a damn that I didn't want him. He demanded food and changed hour by hour, according to the laws of nature, and he was so protected by nature itself that only violence would get rid of him.

"And then we dispatched him with violence."

Her face seemed to have gathered the whole gleam of gray light at the window into its skin. It was alive with a sallow silver tinge while everything else in the living room was dying away in the thinning lamplight. Far away an empty streetcar rushed along. The city was still asleep, but it was as if it had begun to stretch in its slumber.

"Yes, the doctor in our small town was agreeable, just this one time. Johannes had told me that it was nothing, just a trifle, a scraping of the uterus. A trifle? Well, possibly. It didn't hurt very much. No more than you could stand, anyway. But.

"But. How can I express it? Something happens in a woman's body which reminds you daily that something is right. I mean about the fact that you function differently. She has mental aches and pains but she takes nourishment—yes, she's greedy with hunger and displays health and energy like never before. This is normal, you can ask any doctor. There's a lot of self-indulgence and hysteria involved when a woman has to be careful and be paid attention to during pregnancy. You find this sentiment only among those whose lives are such that they are only used to receiving and think the world will come to an end if they're made to contribute something.

"At any rate, what happens is that during pregnancy a woman is protected against her own passions. She can even sleep in spite of anything whatsoever. She's protected because she gives protection herself. She may abuse herself beyond belief; she may run risks to her very life, but nature runs its course in her body, completely oblivious. Every little cell in her body is prepared for what is about to happen.

"And then, suddenly, you perform an act that interrupts this process. In the course of half an hour your heart, kidneys, liver, ovaries, veins and arteries, muscles, nerves, and a million little cells must change. Artificially. With violence. That's it, you see. That's what makes you feel nausea come to your teeth, eyes, fingertips, straight to your marrow as you lie on a stretcher feeling the blood run from what's been torn out of your body and soul during the night in the doctor's office. And he did it for money that he avoided looking at and just threw into a drawer without a word. You look so pale.

"I know I'm being brutal. Men don't like hearing about such things. You *have to* know about it. You have to know what it feels like lying on that bench at the doctor's, enveloped in fear while he digs into you and tears and squeezes and pulls out your uterus. The uterus has no sensation. You feel it in your back, where with abysmal pain he drives one of your organs out of your body and scrapes new life out of it. It's your soul that bleeds during that misdeed. The doctor? I know doctors who've done it for free. He's a victim too, the doctor. He becomes one because he tries to help out with something unbearable. It isn't his fault that it's unbearable. Nor the fault of sinful women or men or of the new life whose permission nobody asked.

"Whose fault, then, is this misdeed? Oh, the perpetrator is invisible. The perpetrator is the judgmental attitude that stones women in trouble and the perpetrator is the fact that food, clothes, warmth, and safety are not a given for every little human being that nature conceived."

○

"Was I asleep? I think I slept a little. You're staring at me. What are you thinking about? Dear, I know what it is. There was something I wanted to tell you. I remember everything. And you'll get to know everything, because now someone has to know everything about me. Yes, I mean about me. But that's not right.

"It isn't just like that. If it concerned only me, it would be inconsequential. No, there's nothing particular about me. What I can tell about myself is neither interesting, nor peculiar and outstanding. No, it has struck me by and by that there are a thousand women affected by this rule of society, this misbegotten rule that is a violation against the laws of nature.

"It comes back to punish you. Violating life itself, I mean. Because all we know of God is the laws of nature, life itself. And we violate life itself. The world has been built crookedly with some kind of arrangement that makes lots of people into hunted animals and a few people so swimmingly well off they can't understand why everybody else isn't happy for them and willing to be beaten to death for their purpose. I think even that is violating life. Nature didn't mean for things to be that way. Nature has enough for everybody. There's something wrong somewhere because on this whole earth there's enough of everything, for everyone.

"But there was something I wanted to tell you, something that happened to Johannes and me before I went to the doctor the second time.

"It happened when I'd made up my mind to stop all that silly running and lifting myself to death and abusing my body to no purpose. He had written me a little note. He hoped everything was fine and I should absolutely write him a few words, write them, yet, telling him how I was doing, and when everything was all right we would have a nice evening together. We would have many nice evenings. It didn't particularly impress me. Well, I was glad he'd written, but it was as if he would just as soon keep me at a distance by saying I should write if something came up.

"I'd begun to feel pretty good again. I was thinking like a human being and I thought, 'No. No. I don't want to. I don't want to do this.' One evening as I was going to bed and had made a good fire in the stove and was washing myself bit by bit in the rusty washbasin, I happened to look at myself in the mirror. I had to look and look. I'd pushed my slip down to my hips and could see that my breasts were beautiful. They sort of glowed. My throat had become fuller and it looked nice. My skin had always been quite problematic. I was used to regarding myself as, well, not pretty, at any rate. But my skin had cleared up, my hair and eyes too, so I looked pretty anyway. And I thought, 'That's the reason. It's because I'm pregnant.' I was standing there falling in love with myself a little. I loved the picture of myself that I saw in the mirror. I caressed my shoulders, which were soft and firm against my cheek. I kissed my arm. If I could have managed I would have kissed my stomach because inside it was the miracle that was happening to me, to the woman who was me. You know, it's really wonderful to be a woman. Or should be. I thought about whether or not it hurt to give birth. I closed my eyes and thought in detail about all I knew about a birth. But I wasn't afraid. Because I was proud and got hot with pride at what women are on this earth to accomplish.

"You see, things like that are those that you experience and remember. Those are the things that stand out and become important and conclusive.

"I was standing there, suddenly warm and happy with a strange and absurd joy. A warm wave of tenderness for everything and everyone made me long to tell Johannes, just tell Johannes something. I don't know. That was all. My eyes wanted to see him and the skin in the palm of my hand wanted to feel the back of his neck and I wanted to tell him about what I was feeling, even though I was far from knowing what that was. So then I got dressed rather than going to bed. I could see that there was a light coming out around Johannes's curtains, a faint reddish light. He was probably working or reading the papers. I could imagine him in his shirt-sleeves. He would be looking up from his work and taking off his glasses and would slowly brighten up when he saw how pretty and happy I was that evening. He would be taking off his glasses and blinking a little and smiling that smile of his. I dawdled for quite a while. I brushed my hair until it shone and buffed my nails.

"It was quite dark outside. The lights from the dock trembled on the dark sea. A few tears trembled in my eyes. I was so fond of everything and everyone and of myself too. A thought made my stomach tighten with cold . . . what would he say when I gave him back the money because I didn't want to go through with it? Maybe I wouldn't say anything, after all. The closer I got to the building the more certain I became that I wouldn't go inside. I just wanted to stand outside his window, knowing he was sitting inside, knowing I loved him. I walked carefully in that crusty snow, preferring to step where footsteps had already bared the ground. I just wanted to be there for a little while, close to him.

"One of the curtains was a little askew. There was a crooked crack that showed some of the shadow play going on in the dimly lit living room. The crack gave me a strange feeling of fear. I felt nauseous and cold, and that strange warm sensation I'd had a short while ago turned into a terrible feeling of weakness that made me tremble and hardly able to stand up. What was the matter with Johannes? I wanted to leave, but it was as if something was hypnotizing me. I stayed nailed to the ground. I thought, 'In a while you'll catch a glimpse of him and then you'll calm down; then all will be well.' And then I caught a glimpse of him."

She broke off and breathed heavily. Her mouth shaped words that didn't emerge. She held her throat with a helpless motion. An engine started up in the courtyard, the sound clattering like shots up the walls. She was startled and listened a bit but retained the listening expression even after the noise had gone, and we could hear nothing but the clock ticking and the rain gossiping in a gutter.

"First his shadow, large and shapeless across the wall, and then Johannes putting on his vest while walking across the room. Then a bit of his jacket that he was putting on.

"And then . . . and then . . . another shadow. Oh, I don't know what was the matter with me but I shipwrecked on the spot. I thought, 'How am I going to get away? How am I going to get away without being heard walking on the snow?'

"If I thought anything at all, that is. Maybe I'm lying a little because my brain was cold as ice and the skin on my head was contracting with a sick cold and I probably wasn't thinking at all. It was a woman. She was hurriedly putting on a coat. She disappeared. I was standing there like a statue, looking at the window with dead eyes. And then Johannes rolled up the curtain, opened the window, and looked out. I don't think any light fell on me; I

107

was standing in the shadow of the balcony, not moving. He called out quite slowly, asking if someone was out there. Then he called out more loudly, angrily. I opened my mouth to answer, but not a sound would come. My lips were dead, made of wood. A freezing and trembling started up in my stomach, like a seizure that shook me through and through; then it quieted down a bit. I wanted to run, flee, disappear. I sat down on the balcony steps where the snow crackled. The steps were not used in winter. Some light fell on me and Johannes said something. I don't remember what he said. The woman came and stood next to him. He put an arm around her shoulders. They couldn't really see who I was, and they were looking to find out. I had to lean my head against the wall. The freezing cold grabbed me by the stomach and my teeth began to chatter. Slowly they spoke to one another. Then she left. I could see her shadow moving on the wall. I think I managed to say who I was because Johannes began to scold, slowly and intensely. He was rude. Well, you know, you just don't do things like that. Walk outside windows. It can only be interpreted as spying. He said something about being a free man. Something about having a private life. What was I to him? What about my private life? There I sat, living my private life outside his window, in the snow. I was dying from privacy. He threatened me, asked me to go away, told me to go on home. I sat. I was shaken by one wave of trembling after the other and couldn't move. I think I asked him to close the window and go back inside. He was furious. He said it was scandalous, that I wanted to scandalize him and ruin him. He said I was the one who had been shining a flashlight into his living room. I hadn't been shining any flashlight. There hadn't been any light from the sea either. It had been dark the whole time. But he and the woman had suddenly seen a strong light at the moment when I was standing out there being run over by inexplicable fear. To this day, he insists that I was shining a strong light on them. That whole thing is really strange.

"I don't know how much time passed. But he came around the corner of the house with his hat and coat on and wanted to take me home. But I couldn't get up. He was malicious. I was shaking like an aspen tree. It felt as if he was kicking open wounds. I noticed that he had been drinking. He lifted me up quite roughly. I had to hold his arm when we left. He dragged me away from that horrible house.

"What had happened began to come alive in my thoughts. It was as if a knife was being turned in my abdomen. Over and over again I experienced that raw pain I'd had outside that window. And at the same time . . . well, what goes on in a human being? By God, that feeling was mixed with the most passionate desire. Of course, I didn't want to; the mere thought made me tremble with screaming disgust. But I didn't dare be alone watching Johannes leave. Would this be the end? He came upstairs with me; I begged him to. He had a bottle of some kind of liqueur along. He had brought it because he needed strength to handle my *betrayal*.

"He said we had to talk. This had to stop. I noticed by and by that he'd had quite a bit to drink. I asked for a drink too. I poured down what I could and felt dizzy and pleasantly dull. A kind of warmth came into me. Alcohol can dull pain. I've used it often. Sometimes I drink with the full knowledge that it's necessary. Every now and then something must be dulled in order to stand living.

"Then he talked to me and it was horrible. He was drunk and drifted between different moods and held me close too. I clung to him then. I didn't want what he thought I wanted. I clung to him with the fear of death and hungrily accepted every caress. He said, sort of apologetically and oblivious of what he was doing to me, that he was already satisfied and couldn't stay. His words tore my stomach open and closed my throat, but I didn't dare be alone and asked him not to leave. Have you ever heard it said that the last thing a human being clings to is the executioner? What do we want him for? Well, well, I don't know. To find our humanity, maybe, our *common* humanity. What is the difference between pride and humility? Pride is nothing but admiration, respect, and love for one's own self being bigger than love for another. And humility comes from giving so unreasonably much more than you're capable of.

"He didn't leave. We slept together. He slept, that is. I lay there getting sober. Everything in me was black with pain. I felt his breath. He had the scent of another woman on him. I gently touched his face and loved every one of his features and cried. Later on he took me, before he left. With a lascivious hangover embrace. I was what he wanted me to be.

"I think deep down he liked the situation. There's a lot left of the ape in us. Because I too, I, well, I was that way, I participated completely.

"I loved him with a monstrous passion. After he left I felt as if everything good in me had been killed.

"The next evening I went to the doctor and had it done. That which some people call a trifle."

◗

"What time is it now? Oh, it's late. I don't have much time. Here comes that damned nervousness again. No, I'll hurry up, but you mustn't be impatient. Oh God, I have to get it all said, but I'm in a hurry."

She doubled up in the chair and clenched her fists against her face. She groaned a little and I could see that her forehead got shiny gray with sweat. I poured wine into her glass. She took it hesitantly. Her hand was

111

shaking a little. She put it down without drinking and turned her face away. It was drawn with pain.

"Yes. That was that. I was through with Johannes. Well, I told myself every day that I was through with Johannes. I stayed in bed for a few days that time but not for long enough. The thought that I had to get back to my job would not let me rest in peace. It was a temporary thing and there was no insurance and I was afraid of poverty. There was a lot of unemployment then, you know. But I felt sick and bad and would turn away whenever I saw children playing in the street.

"I got a curtain for my window so I could avoid seeing whether or not there was a light on at Johannes's. But it sometimes happened that I was driven out of bed at night to move the curtain and look. When it was dark I felt an aching tenderness because at least he was alone then, I thought. When there was a light on, my teeth froze and I relived all that had happened and I killed it over and over again.

"I was through with Johannes. But every once in a while he would come into the shop to buy cigarettes. I'd give the wrong change and behave like a fool, but I wouldn't look at Johannes because I was through with him.

"There were never many guests at Nilsen's hotel. There was a dining room and an old fashioned drawing room in plush with a column covered with Thorvaldsen's painting of Christ, and a small organ. Salesmen came there mostly, often the same ones. One of them was named Mohn. To this day I don't know his first name. He chased me a few times, but nicely. He asked my forgiveness and asked if I was angry. He was lonely. A salesman's life is lonely and sordid. I was lonely myself and didn't get angry. He was a stationary salesman, and he gave me a box of pink writing paper with a pansy at the top of the sheet. His hands were too white and his nails were not always quite clean. There was something unpleasant about his face, I can't say what it was. He was very handsome, too handsome, but there was something disgusting about his mouth. I didn't like him and felt sorry for him because it was completely impossible to like him. This wasn't it . . . I'm talking nonsense and I'm in a hurry.

"Well, sometimes I'd go up to The Mine too. My sister had gotten married. My mother and brother had had to move out of the house, which was a wreck of a house anyway, old and uncomfortable. She had to go to work; she did laundry. My brother had quit grammar school and had gotten a job at the cannery where my sister used to work. He was just a boy and got thirty-five øre an hour during the season. Most of it went for bus fare. But there was a possibility of permanent employment at the factory; besides there wasn't anything else. But my mother, well, I couldn't take it. Sometimes I'd turn around and go back down without going to see her.

"You see, it wasn't just that she'd gotten run down in her clothes and appearance. She had lost all her upper teeth; they'd been pulled out and she couldn't afford to have new ones put in. She was too tired when she came home from work to fix herself up. Her hair was tattered, she had spots of soot up along her arms from the laundry kettles, and her hands were swollen red and so waterlogged it hurt to look at them. The worst part was . . . well, the part that made me notice *how* reduced she was, was the way she talked. She drank coffee constantly and only talked about other people. Her eyes had acquired a vindictive glint whenever she would talk about the things she was part of in the families for whom she did the wash, kitchen gossip and the like, all ears. And using her eyes. Oh God, what is it about poverty? Is it the lack of happy events? Is it the soul's hunger for a circus? Is it that other people's misery and humiliation give some the feeling that after all . . . oh, shoot, what a sleazy satisfaction. I would just as soon not have gone home. I didn't feel bound to anyone, family ties or anything like that. But there was something else, almost as painful, well, just as painful, what am I saying . . . more painful than anything else. It was the pleasure that surfaced on these two faces when I brought something. A bag of buns. My mother would dip them in her coffee with a kind of relish that forced me to look away.

"A few ounces of real butter, two eggs. And that expectation when I got things out of my bag. She would talk about this and that and try not to look at the bag. And my brother. He sat in the corner in the twilight by the cookstove. He was dirty and pale and there was something old in his face. Fourteen. I would bring him an orange, but he was ashamed and said I should have it. His eyes shone in all the dirt and he held the orange and licked the peel. He put it up on the mantel to make it shine, then he took it down and enjoyed it, eating little pieces of the peel to save the expensive fruit and keep it for a long time. Do you understand this, can you understand any of this? Do you comprehend that it was their joy I could stand least of all?

"All this, you see, all this weighed heavy and poisonous on top of everything that made my own life heavy to carry around at that time. It had gotten so that it was painful to exist, even though I wasn't thinking. I had some sort of bad conscience that I couldn't really locate anywhere or know how to handle. There was something I ought to have done but didn't have time for, something I was neglecting. It took away my sleep; one thing after the other, I would lie there aching.

"Oh well, I can't really remember what I wanted to tell you by saying this, but it was something important and now I can't remember it. But it was something very conclusive. Well, well, it'll probably come to me. I'm just so nervous. I have to go soon; I know I don't have much time.

"You see, every living minute was a minute of pain. It felt like a physical pain eating away at me, and it can affect one's health. I was managing well with the seventeen kroner I received every Saturday afternoon at Madsen's Tobacco and I had free room and board and worked a bit at the hotel. But I was sick and tired of these rooms with their wine bottles in the corners and their indeterminate smells and the pursuits of salesmen who thought they would have themselves a little adventure. There wasn't any convincing pursuit anyway. I was really ugly during that period. I noticed it whenever I tried going to a dance or something. Nobody asked me to dance. My throat became stringy with leanness. I rarely looked in a mirror and became careless about my appearance.

"When the snow began to smell of spring and all the trees became expectant and the sparrows started to go crazy in the sunshine, I ached as though I had a boil inside, night and day. Sometimes I'd see Johannes and all my strength would sort of leave me. I would sneak out of the way to avoid him. I was, by all means, completely through with him.

"The evenings began to stay lighter and then I'd take the trip up to The Mine. On Sundays I'd take long lonely walks, preferably to places where I wouldn't meet boys and girls holding hands. There were things I'd seen year in and year out that appeared new and strange and painful to me. It was beautiful, too, but I was in turmoil what with this interminable spring, you know. There are small friendly farms around our town. Forest and rock and a boathouse in every bay in the fjord. There were dung heaps in the snow and the fields were yellow in places. There was a smell of burnt peat and the sheep were out finding a few things to eat. The very first lambs had begun to arrive.

"Lambs are always cute and funny, you know, but all this budding life struck me differently then. One Sunday I took a detour up to The Mine. The sun hurt my eyes; I tired quickly and had to rest a few times. There were a few sheep chewing away and looking at me thoughtfully. It's quite incredible how thoughtful a sheep can look. They quite forget to chew from sheer thoughtfulness. But you know, there were a few lambs. They were crazy with delight over being in this world. They ran away with awkward jumps and their mother came grumbling after, reminding them not to run away. There's a whole world of tenderness and wisdom in such a coarse sheep's voice. Then they'd run behind the rocks and hide anyway, getting terribly surprised and instantly hungry when they could no longer see their mother and would call her with a ridiculous thin bleating. Oh my, oh my! And she answered. She was chewing and calling back in her coarse and rumbling voice. It sounded like she was talking because she was chewing. It was a play I'd seen many times, but I was seeing it for the first time. The two little nincompoops were running around in circles and around the rocks and had gotten completely turned around. They were squeaking and crying and the mother was bellowing and scolding. All the other sheep entered the conversation with their different voices. There was a scent of growth from the earth. I felt my nails digging into it and my hand get full of grainy snow and tufts of grass and earth. Finally they discovered their mother and careened crazily toward her and ran straight into her stomach and bumped it, shaking their tails in ecstasy. And the mother started nibbling on the tufts of grass again, calmly and happily chewing and grumbling a little from time to time. She lifted her head like an Egyptian queen and looked at me and quite distinctly said, 'Look at me, you idiot.'

"I felt a pain in my lip, I was chewing it. A string sort of burst inside me, a string that had been too taut for too long. Something was squeezing my heart to the point of bursting. There was a circus going on with those greedy lambs. I laughed. Yes, I was convinced I was chuckling and laughing.

"Then I discovered I was crying my heart out."

"In the long run a human being cannot stand being all alone. I'd gotten completely away from my girl friends at The Mine and when in town they didn't really want to say hello to me. I don't know why, but I'd probably gotten a bad reputation. I was no different than anyone else. I longed for someone who would be good to me, that there would be a man whom I could be good to. I don't think there was a question of erotic love or anything; I was so young and new and I could never think of such things with anyone but Johannes, and then only with a burning pain. And still, still. I started getting a little pleased every time the salesman named Mohn came by, not because I liked him, but because he liked me. He showed a kind of tenderness toward me and there was a warmth to his eyes and voice. I began to find him pleasant.

"Sometimes I'd meet Johannes. Have I told you what Johannes looks like? No, it's impossible to describe, you see, but there is something about him, something . . . : well, he always looks as if his hands are cold. He has such worried hands. One day when there was no one else there he came to the shop. I was neither unsure nor stupid that day because Mohn had arrived during the night and in the morning there was a package outside my door. It was a small box with a picture of a kitty on the outside and a silly little note 'from someone well known, but unnoticed.'

"Well, it was nothing, but something anyway. I don't know if you'll understand. But anyway, Johannes looked at me with that old tenderness in his eyes and I recognized his eyebrows and those worried hands and did not feel ashamed that I almost had tears in my eyes. I even smiled at him and asked how he was doing. He had a bit of a cold and Johannes is such that he appeals to an unfortunate tenderness in women. I gave him a little calendar because I couldn't embrace him and put my mouth against his eyebrows or place his hand against my cheek. He got so pleased with that idiotic little calendar, turning the pages with those hands of his. You've never seen Johannes when his eyes turn happy under his eyebrows.

"No, I'm being terribly silly, you see; there's no continuity to what I'm telling you. But that time was a mess. And I have to tell this the way it comes to me because I have to tell it all before I go. What time is it?"

I nodded my head toward the clock on the mantel. She looked at it and pulled her coat more tightly around her. Intermittent footsteps sounded on the sidewalks outside and from the courtyard you could hear a merry whistling bouncing off the walls of the building. A door banged and a drunk was singing somewhere.

"Once in a while I'd go to the sports center when there was a dance, for a bit of fun. But the fun never materialized. Nobody wanted to dance with me other than the slouches no one else wanted. There was a bit of drinking going on. As the evening wore on some of the older people would come to find drinking companions and to stand in a group in the hall, talking. One of the people who came often was our organist. No one ever saw him drink, but he was always stiff with liquor. He was somewhat of a strange one. Everyone knew he drank but he always stayed upright, and he was an unusually accomplished musician. Sometimes he would go to the church at night and play all by himself. You can imagine how strange it was to walk past the prim white church, roaring among the empty graves. The church was right by the water's edge and the sea hummed around the inlet and the church stood alone exuding music. The organist talked like a sensible human being when he was drunk; otherwise he never said a word. Sometimes he sat down next to me at the sports center and talked to me. He gave me much to think about. He was very, very lonely. Being with him made me feel less lonely. He looked at me with one blue and one brown eye and asked me why I was pining away. I couldn't really tell him why. But why am I talking about him now? Well, there must be a reason.

"Johannes had started coming into the store more frequently. He would look through magazines and find something to do until the other customers had been taken care of and we were alone. Whenever he'd been there talking to me for a while about nothing at all I would hum and weigh out too much candy for the children who came around. One day he said, 'It's been a long time. I've missed you.'

"That's all it took. I got completely lost in those words and let them sing inside me and lived off them. And I thought he cared about me a little at any rate and that all would be well. In all seriousness, I fooled myself this way. It doesn't take much for someone who's always troubled. Once in a while I'd meet him outside and he'd smile and say hello. There's a certain light across Johannes's forehead when he smiles.

"One day I met him on my way up to The Mine. It was a bright spring evening. There was one star in the sky and a crescent moon of pale silver hanging above the treetops. Birds were whistling a lonely tearful music in the birch forest where the trees were dreaming in a mist of bursting buds and the pond reflected the last blue light from a dying sky. Well, it was the kind of evening that made him turn around and accompany me for a while. Think of it, there were even some people on the road at times and everything. His voice was warm and young and happy. And he said, 'Just imagine the two of us taking another trip.' He said, 'Everything is different when we get away from this town.' Well, we talked a whole lot. It was nice and intimate, and I don't know how it happened but I asked him or teased him . . . well, I wanted to extract from him whether or not there was another woman seriously involved. He said that was just nonsense, don't listen to that kind of talk. He still couldn't get married because he didn't make enough money and needed to finish his education. And I got happy. For that reason. And I couldn't hide my happiness, so much so that he finally pulled me into the woods and afterwards he whispered into my mouth that there were just the two of us, just him and me, and that he loved me. We brushed pine needles and things off each other and fooled around, laughing. I was beyond sense and reason.

"I kissed him as we parted. Right in the middle of the country road where the new moon cast pale shadows I kissed him and asked if I was really no longer supposed to come to his place. Because I'd seen something in his eyes, something like a little shadow of worry, while he had a smoke sitting on a tree stump before we went back to the road.

"He just said that everything would get better if we could go away for a while and be by ourselves and that we would do so some time. I groaned with hot delight at his saying this. But I asked him if we couldn't be together on my birthday, which was coming up soon. I would be eighteen then. He smiled and said he'd see about that. He looked at his watch. We parted.

"The following days were strange because I was looking forward and felt uncertain. I was happy, unhappy, restless and nervous, back in the same old thing . . . thinking only about Johannes. I bought a half bottle of wine and some fruit. I wanted to ask him to come to my room. He could come after the others in the building had gone to bed and we could have a nice evening by ourselves. He came into the shop the day before my birthday and then I invited him. He thought about it and said he'd try to make it. I said he had to come for sure and he nodded and smiled before he left, but he was sort of absent-minded, which I didn't especially notice then but came to think about later.

"But he'd promised to come and I was looking forward, mixed with flutters of fear sharp as steel. But he had promised. I bought flowers that fixed up the sorry room and half borrowed, half stole a nice tablecloth from Mrs. Nilsen with which to set the table. In the evening I was sick with impatience and thought that time crept along slowly. I was afraid he'd come before the others went to bed. I fluttered around my room, brushed my hair, rearranged the fruit, moved the flowers from one spot to another, and started to listen. Because the building had become quiet. The moon was shooting little silent lightning glances down into the rocks at the tideline. The sea was like velvet. It was so quiet and I listened for his footsteps. Then fear started chopping bloody little chips out of my happiness. But he'd promised to come, he probably would. My palms were damp. In the street that I could see from my window he'd have to pass a streetlight as he walked. I stared that way and repeatedly thought I saw him coming, but it wasn't him; sometimes it wasn't anybody. From time to time I knew with the glimmer of blind pain, 'He's not coming.' But I choked that down and thought I heard footsteps. It was only the sea at the tideline. Every minute that passed lasted a year and I told myself that the reason was my looking forward so much and being impatient. I had on a new white collar for my dress and had to check in the mirror to see if I looked pretty for him, but I wasn't pretty because my eyes were two black caverns in a flat gray white plane. He'd turned out the light in his window a long time ago and I thought he'd probably ended up talking with someone on his way down. The fear finally settled like a permanent ache. Every minute was like a year of torture."

A locomotive hooted angrily. Someone's dragging footsteps could be heard on the staircase, along with newspapers clashing into maildrops up and down the entry doors in the building. There was a hammering of steel and the growling sound of a machine coming from the factory. More and more often, boots clattered on the sidewalk. The cigarette smoke that was floating up under the ceiling shone with a weak silver shimmer, and the lamplight was powerless.

"The moon began to shoot stars across the sea. After a while there was an entire firework and little by little the moon gathered the firework together into a large shimmering river that paled into the night and split apart and disappeared. At Johannes's the light went on once again. And died a while later. Day was breaking, a rooster crowed. When I looked at myself in the mirror to take off my pretty white collar, my face was dry and my eyes completely colorless.

"Days passed once more, sick, heavy days. I was ashamed and depressed. Johannes came into the shop but there were other customers and I felt crushed by nervousness while he was there. He barely looked at me, he seemed maybe ashamed; there was sort of a helplessness about him. I'm not bitter toward Johannes. He's a human being.

"I couldn't stand thinking about him. I went to the sports center, almost just to have a talk with the gray-haired organist, should he show up. I wanted to ask him to take a walk with me. I wanted to listen to him. I wanted to think about everything he said and not just about Johannes.

"We were talking; *he* talked, that is, but I was restless and depressed and not really listening to what he was saying. And then he looked at me and said, 'It's a shame, a bloody shame.' He said, 'Here you are getting ruined.' And that . . . that I couldn't stand hearing. His interest, his seriousness, no, it made me utterly desperate. I asked him to take a walk with me, and we went to my place and drank all the wine I'd bought for my birthday when Johannes didn't come. I drank quite deeply. I wasn't used to it and I felt the wine like a flame in my chest and stomach and then my head started getting funny. I laughed a little and then I cried. But Morck just looked at me. There was such a seriousness about him. He said, 'Good God. Good God, girl, what have they done to you?' Morck had one blue and one brown eye and they always looked sober, even when he was drunk. I had expected him to be different; maybe I expected him to embrace me or something, but Morck wasn't that way. It got pretty silly and we drank a toast and I told him he was my only friend. Which he really was too.

"We drank the half bottle. I sang a sad little tune about love for him, laughing and crying and behaving strangely. He remained serious. 'Good Lord, child,' he said. Then I had to go out for a walk. He put on his hat and scarf without a word. We left. I was a bit unsteady on the stairs and held his arm. Mohn was just coming up the stairs and I gave him a cheerful greeting. He looked at us.

"The moon was almost full. It was a nice evening. I felt that the wine had done me good and relieved some of the pressure I felt. But I worried about tomorrow and was whimpering a little in my fear of tomorrow, which would be a worse day than ever. Morck asked if I liked music and if he could play some for me. He said it was better than wine and I was grateful.

"We let ourselves into the church, which was bathed in moonlight. We lit no lights and our steps sang out, even though we walked very carefully.

"It was strange entering the empty church. It smelled of woodwork, masonry, candle wax, and dust inside. It was like any empty house. The moon shone through the window in the choir and cast its light in white runners, crookedly covering the benches. We could see the whole empty church, the empty pulpit, and all the empty benches. Morck was standing next to me. He looked at me and asked what I was thinking. His voice echoed in the empty space around us. I just shook my head because I didn't know what I was thinking. He asked how I felt being in the empty church but I just shook my head at that too. Breathing heavily, he said that he, on his part, felt solemn. He felt a tenderness for the empty benches and the few psalm books here and there and for the worn stairs. He said he didn't believe in God. But he believed in people. I had to look at him then because the people in that town were not particularly nice to him. They spoke badly of him and froze him out. He had no other friends than the organ, the bottle, and me.

"He was speaking quite slowly and said he could bow down deeply on behalf of this room because this was where people deposited all their capacities for love, and those were really quite powerful. I felt my inebriation fall away, and I don't know, but I had to look at him to make sure he was serious. I was caught in a feeling of discomfort because I wondered if he was a bit mad. He said, 'This is where the poor find riches, where the weak find strength. This is where the scared find their hope. Don't you have to bow your head to a power that can give people riches that don't exist and strength that weakens their solidarity and hope that removes all hope in this life?' Well, I really became a little frightened of him, he was so serious and moved. He said, 'I love people for their simplicity. I love them for their poverty. I love them for the fear that oppresses them. And now I'll play for you.'

"And then he sat down at the organ and played all those psalms that I loved, "A Mighty Fortress Is Our God," "Rock of Ages"—well, that's a song I like a lot, but I don't know anything about music. What he played felt nice and soft to me. The darkness in the church shimmered like mother-of-pearl. I hid away in the darkest corner of the choir and cried. They were good tears. The moon, which had been shining in at an angle, was shining straight down now, making the church lighter inside. I could see the altarpiece I liked so much. After he'd played for a while he suddenly broke off and said something. I jumped because he was no longer lowering his voice; it hit me from all the walls. He said, 'And now I'll play something different for you, something quite different.'"

She was turning her glass around in her hands and attentively examining the pale reflections playing in the red wine. A cart rattled through the street outside, and somewhere in the building someone slammed a door. She slowly put the glass to her mouth and drank.

"He said, 'Now I'll perform the riches which are human rights and the strength which is hidden in them and the hope which will put that strength to use. Yes, I'll perform defiance and rebellion and that reality where human happiness resides, waiting for human beings to grab it, take it themselves. They must take it themselves!'

"As he said the last words, his fists were clenched and his voice cracked. Then it was quiet for a long time. I could see only that he was hunched forward over the organ and I don't know if he was crying. It was so quiet, the whole church was listening. Then he said in a subdued and suspended voice, I had to hold my breath to hear, 'And I'll perform my infirmity for you. I'll perform the reason I drink.'

"Then the whole church began to roar. There was a storm of harmonies. I had to get up and walk all around the choir. He was playing full force with passionate earnestness and the music was coming from the ceiling, from the pulpit, from all the walls. There was a flaming and burning of music, like a blood red vortex. As if the whole church was on fire. It was wonderful! Struggle and longing and happiness, well, I can't describe it. But I felt strong all of a sudden, suffused by a strength I hadn't known. It was too strong to carry alone. I wished the church was full of people. I could almost see them dressed in black on all the benches. They grew out of the moonlit dust in front of me and they lifted their heads, they listened, they stood up. They grew and were holding hands. They became a dense mass that got thicker and grew and wandered straight across all the benches and everything, a solid wall of people walking toward the same goal with a strength that . . . well, with the same strength that enabled me to stand there in the lonely choir as if I were on fire, with hands so tightly clenched I had a hard time opening them afterwards. It was nonsense, of course, but the words he had spoken that I didn't understand much of and the music, this rhythmic sea of flames that undulated like a fire . . . oh, I just don't know. It was a wonderful experience. And real. I didn't see any visions or anything; it all happened inside me and it was beautiful because it was real. At the moment when I thought all the people were streaming down and disappearing by the altarpiece I realized it was all because the moonlight through the windows had shifted once again and was falling at an angle so that it hit the altarpiece straight on and made its colors stand out like jewels. The visible parts of Christ were just the face full of suffering, struggle, and defiance and his naked arm being lifted by those who carried him. One of them wore a red shirt and it shone like a blood red banner in the hand of Christ. There was something triumphant about him now that you couldn't see he'd been crucified. Well, there I was breathless and hot and letting the music conjure unknown forces in my soul. I no longer gave Johannes a single thought, the way I had while I was crying over the psalms.

"When the music stopped we could hear the sea beating down at the beach. It sounded like little tingling pieces of ice being crushed on the rocks. I felt the rhythm of my heart throughout my body, and my hands were so tightly clenched they were like stuck in a cramp. Morck sat for a long time, bent over the keys.

"I almost thought he'd fallen asleep, so I went over and touched his shoulder. He looked up with a start and I noticed then that Morck was an old man. But his eyes were certainly awake. We didn't exchange a single word as long as we stayed in the church. When we were outside and he was locking the door, I asked him quite gently what that piece he had played for me was called. He told me it was Bach's *Toccata and Fugue in D Minor* but that didn't mean a thing to me, so I said nothing.

"It was a wonderful night out. Morck's voice was hoarse and strange when he said that he was sober now and that he had to hurry home to get a little drunk before he turned in. Then I remembered what he'd said about wanting to perform for me, about why he drank. And I asked what he'd really meant by that. He just shrugged his shoulders and said he was merely the Lord's poor fiddler. I thought he must be a little crazy. But I felt a deep tenderness for him and I thought I'd better say something so that he wouldn't notice my thinking he was crazy. The area and the town lay frozen in a wild, white moonlight and I would just as soon have been silent about it and not ruined it with words, but I said something about it being beautiful. He looked at me then with a little smile, filled with bitterness. He looked at the moon and at me and said in a voice tired as death: 'Human beings have a weakness for moonlight. It doesn't blind them. It doesn't burn them.'

"Then we walked in silence for a long time. When we parted he said: 'Nothing grows by moonlight.' "

"Well, maybe you think it's strange that I talk about this organist. He had nothing to do with me. Be that as it may, I feel I have to tell about him anyway. He went off and killed himself one day. He gave me something that night in the church and, had I only understood the implications, maybe everything would have turned out differently.

"Some of the strength I experienced that night stayed with

me. That's what made me start to think about the future. I really wanted to learn something and I had to have something permanent to earn money on so that I didn't have to continue cleaning those rooms. That was the kind of work I didn't like; I never have. Mrs. Nilsen had started being cool toward me, probably something to do with my reputation. I felt this coolness everywhere. I think it was probably because of the organist.

"Mohn had changed too. He waited for me in the dark hallway and grabbed me, but I twisted away and didn't want to make a fuss, because of Mrs. Nilsen. One evening he invited me for a glass of wine in his room, but I said no thanks. 'In the living room then,' he said. I said no thanks. He looked a bit forlorn and I thought I hadn't needed to reject him quite so much. He probably was well-meaning. He'd given me little gifts.

"It was strange about Johannes. He was my big weakness and I sometimes thought I'd better be through with him once and for all and get going on something. What I really meant by 'get going' wasn't clear to me, but I felt I had strength. The roads had become muddy, the snow had gone, the thrushes had arrived, they rejoiced throughout the woods. I thought I would talk to Johannes about what I should do. I wanted to learn something and use my strength for something.

"I told him this one day when he came into the shop. It felt good to know I could talk to him about such reasonable things. He was my teacher once again, the thoughtful teacher who remembered I'd been a good student and had a talent for languages and history. He said that I ought to have continued my studies. That I had deserved to go to the gymnasium. I blushed with happiness at the fact that he was saying this and I thought that if I would learn something and make something of myself I wouldn't be 'just anyone' that he couldn't possibly marry. But it would cost money.

"It felt good to talk to him about it. It warmed my heart to feel his interest. Well, anyway, that's the way he was toward everybody. He was very nice and liked by everyone. That's the essential part of Johannes, his goodness. But he has a weakness for women. That's often the case with the best of men; they have such a weakness for women that they turn out to be disasters, and malicious without wanting to be.

"I realized I was still hopelessly fond of him. But I'd come to terms with things being the way they were and I wanted to work. I had to see to it that I got a job where I could use my abilities. And Johannes showed me that he wished me the best. He brought me books that he let me borrow and showed that he had been thinking about me. I fondled those books and had myself a good yearning time. I whispered, 'my Johannes.' Being his girl bound me to him and I accepted being tied to him without binding him. It was possible to be alone without anxiety when I had his books. I had greatly enjoyed reading biographies, things I'd found on my own. I'd been able to borrow books from someone where a friend of mine worked. She was the one who showed me the *Decameron*. She thought it was so terrible that she read it all the time. It was the first significant book I held in my hand.

"So I got to know about kings and statesmen, about rulers who for many generations had been in the hands of political speculators, about people who starved and toiled, about anonymous women who had power over those who held power—beautiful, stupid, devious, relentless women who had ruled men for years and years. And masses of people who had toiled for them and bled for them and gone to war for them for years and years. I took to sitting up into the night, thinking about how it could be that beautiful empty-headed women could bring about the fall of entire populations and feed off the poverty of the people.

"Well, I thought more than I read. I thought about my mother and her bloody struggles and about all the new little humans who every day were not allowed into the world, and about the tragedy of the crowned ones, who were just pawns in purple and ermine who were not allowed to be human, and who were always unhappy. I had to pace the floor, as far as the space allowed, because of a brewing unrest that agitated me. What I learned posed ever more questions and led my thoughts back to my own situation, to my own time and to everything around me. I burned to talk to Johannes about all this. But when I mentioned it to him one day at the shop he laughed at me and said, 'I didn't know you were a revolutionary.' He didn't understand me. I could have wept. It meant so much to me to have him, in particular, understand what was at work in me, that which I barely understood myself.

"I asked him what he thought when he read these books. He said they were interesting. I could have spit in his face with annoyance. For a person has to realize that what's interesting about history is what it has to teach us about our own times, right? But you don't hear a word about that in school. That's why it all became new to me when I'd gained some experience and could think on my own.

"But an activity had been started in my brain that I could neither handle nor explain. I sent my whole week's wages up to my mother and felt painfully ashamed afterwards. Because it didn't alter a single thing. Everything got all mixed up, you see. When I read about a queen giving insanely expensive parties to fill the emptiness in her existence and to be paid for by the animal labor of peasants, I would think about the fireworks we could see coming from the summer estates of the rich from the bigger cities, estates that sprang up like mushrooms during the war. And I would think about the anxiety-filled fireworks we could barely see out in the ocean at that time. I mixed the luxury and delights of a queen's pleasure palace with the anxiety of the whip wielded over peasants who had to pay most of their crops in taxes so that the queen could pay her gambling debts. And everybody, but everybody agreed that the revolution was right because it had happened in the olden days, a long time ago. The same people could not comprehend that the same thing was now repeating itself because those who died in the fire out in the ocean were also those who paid for the champagne parties held in the summer estates whose beautiful fireworks we could see. Well, it felt as if it was happening right outside my living room door, all that stuff about the peasants, without my being able to lift a finger to change it.

"The peasants and workers who were bled by the frivolous queen and the clever statesmen revolted and blood flowed. I cried for the queen who was taken to the gallows without understanding she'd done something wrong. I thought that she was just stupid and really a harmless person. She wasn't allowed to be a human being because she was a pawn and she didn't know what it meant to go wanting and didn't understand what her frivolity cost in terms of human suffering.

"Luxury liners passed in the fjord at night. They glittered like jewels and we could hear the music on board. But the newspapers said there was more and more unemployment everywhere, and people dead on park benches in the morning.

"There were strikes and unrest all over the world. There had been revolutions and upheavals; nevertheless things remained the same. There had to be something wrong with these upheavals, something missing. In Russia there had just been the biggest revolution of all time, but I couldn't make heads or tails out of what the newspapers were saying about this. I understood the revolution to still be going on, but some papers wrote about it as if it was all said and done and that was that. And it was a horrible thing, from what I could understand. No, it was impossible to figure anything out. Sometimes I just wanted to give up on everything. But I couldn't get rid of the feeling that it concerned me, all of it concerned me, and all of it concerned everything else. None of what happened could be understood without your understanding the whole thing. Well, my head got hot with all this thinking that was taking hold of me, and I was aglow with the music Morck had played for me that night. I didn't remember other than bits and pieces and got impatient with the fact that I couldn't find all the notes. Just the way I got impatient with not getting the totality of what I was forced to think about and was not able to dismiss.

"One night I got it into my head that I had to hear that music again, immediately. I had the feeling it would fix my whirlwind of thoughts if I could hear that music again, hear it in the church where the air was heavy with all the big sorrows that people had left behind but that didn't get smaller from having been left. So I got dressed. I wanted to see if there was a light on at Morck's. It was one o'clock in the morning.

"It was raining outside, a mild and growth-laden rain. The fields around town and the bursting birch forest smelled strongly. The sea was singing down at the beach. I was full of hot longing for my Johannes, which drove me more quickly toward Morck. I was a tangle of thoughts I had to get fixed. I felt possessed by an enormous, unhappy, urgent love.

"Then I saw him. Johannes. He was standing alone in the rain outside the pharmacist's house. He was standing some distance away from the streetlight, in the dark. A gray unmoving figure. My heart shrank. I don't know, I had a choking sense of tenderness. His hat was pulled down over his face, his scarf was up over his ears. But I recognized him from what little I could see of him. I would recognize him forever, he was my Johannes. I couldn't help him. I sneaked past. I ran. I didn't want to think about him any more. It was useless thinking myself to death about him.

"There was a light on at Morck's. He lived above a garage, alone. I'd never been there before. No one ever visited Morck.

"I heard him singing and humming in there. He got quieter when I knocked, but he didn't say 'come in.' I heard some glasses slowly clinking. The door was locked. I knocked again and it got completely quiet and then he finally cracked the door. I must have looked strange because he opened the door wide and asked if something had happened to me. I just asked if I could please come inside. There was a gust of wine on his breath. He was much too steady when he went to find a chair and he had to clear the mess off it first. I was pretty surprised because I had not known that he had a grand piano. It was covered with clothes and things and thick with dust. A chest of drawers was standing there with all its drawers open. The bed was not made. There was a sour smell of old tobacco, wine, and sweat. He sat there dressed in a tattered sweater and he had loosened his shirt collar, which hung down crookedly.

"I didn't know what to say. My head was in complete confusion. What had happened to all the things I wanted to tell him? To ask him about? He was leaning forward with his elbows on his knees, looking at me. I felt he was looking straight through me, even though he was so drunk his head was swaying. I saw the picture of Johannes's lonely gray figure in the rain and had to hug myself in my sense of helplessness.

"After a long while Morck asked if he could offer me something and then I somehow managed to say that I hoped he would bring me to the church again and play like last time. But I no longer sounded convincing. The ardent feeling of having found a groove that was leading me forward had become cluttered. I thought, 'Maybe Johannes was waiting for someone.'

"Morck just shook his head. No, he didn't want to play any organ. I darkened with indistinct hopelessness. I begged him to do it anyway. I imagined that there would be some kind of salvation in his playing again and that it would put me in the same state of strength as earlier. And now I even had more, even more that I had thought about, and I tried to explain this to him. I think it must have sounded foolish because I was crying from time to time and couldn't make heads or tails out of what was stirring in me. Morck's hands were limply hanging down over his knees. There was something unfeeling and alien about his sitting like that. His torso was swaying. His brown and his blue eye were looking at me from two separate worlds. He was two people staring at me. He said, 'Another time, another time. I'll play another time.'

"So I stayed a while, out of politeness. Didn't feel I could get up and leave right away. I thought, 'Maybe Johannes is still standing there, maybe he's alone.' I was cold and I said I didn't know Morck had a grand piano, wasn't such a grand piano expensive? He hummed a little, saying it was quite expensive. 'I've signed my human worth away to the devil for that grand piano.' I sadly thought he was drunk, too drunk. I was alone. And I didn't notice that he'd gotten up until he opened the cover with a bang and swore a little. He pulled up a chair and managed to sit down with a great deal of hubbub, which gave me the worst kinds of ideas. But once he'd found his place he sat completely still until it was quiet. I could hear the rain breathing around the house and my own heartbeats.

"And then he played. The silence melted away. The music was so wary and so tender and so certain, as if he'd never had a drop to drink. He played something that was melancholy and light at the same time. It was like wine. It was a good moment. So full of longing, but good. Oh, I was loving the grand piano and the dirty apartment and the rain outside. I loved myself and Morck's long, faded figure sitting there at the piano making magic. But when Johannes touched my thoughts, pain would tie me up inside. I pushed him away because it was too much to take. When Morck stopped playing, the silence hit me like a cold darkness. He was looking at me. He said, 'I think you need a glass of wine. You're cold. Dry your tears.'

"I didn't know I was crying, because I wasn't really crying. There were just tears flowing freely from my eyes. But my heart was shivering and my lips were cold.

"I accepted the wine greedily. He didn't drink. He put the cork in the bottle and watched me drink. Then he sat down and rolled a cigarette. I asked for a cigarette too. He gave me the one he'd rolled and fished out a butt from somewhere under his sweater for himself.

"I said that the wine did me good. He was smoking and looking at me from under his eyebrows. He said, 'Be careful.' Much later he said, 'The bottle is a good friend to the one who treats it well and a false friend to the one who thinks he can offer it anything.' Then he shut up and I was beginning to have a nice time. I thought that wine was kind, peaceful, and warm for someone who was afraid. The cigarette made me a little dizzy at first but it cleared up my thoughts. I started talking after a while, and I thought that what I was saying was wise and reasonable. I talked about all the things I'd thought about and that I needed to talk to someone about. But Morck was in his own world. He said, 'Be careful. You should only drink alone and only when you can't stand it otherwise. Not with just anybody. Never in bad company.' Well, well, that was all right, but I wanted to talk about me. The wine was sweet and good, cool in my throat and warm in my stomach. I asked him why the majority of people put up with their misery when, after all, there had to be a way to make a good life. He said, 'You can drink with me. But don't drink with anybody else.' I said, 'Why don't they rebel, why don't they lance the boil?' He poured more wine for me and asked me to promise never to drink wine with just anybody. We were talking on either side of an invisible brick wall. There was just nonsense going on and at last I asked desperately, 'You said you'd signed away your human worth to the devil. What did you mean by that?'

"He got up. He rolled a cigarette, walked a few paces, sat down again with his head bent. He said, 'I've heard everything you've said.'

"I'm assuring you, he was completely sober. If I hadn't smelled him when I first came, I would have thought he hadn't had anything to drink at all. Then he talked about himself.

"About an hour later, when I left, he was sitting with his head on his arm at the table. The bottle he'd just emptied was hanging from his hand. He was whimpering into his arm, but he wasn't crying.

"It had stopped raining. The rain had absorbed all the dense spring freshness from the darkness and a golden melody from a bird's throat shone across the hills. It seemed so overwhelming after the confined apartment and the remarkable things the organist had told about. I drank in the freshness of the night with closed eyes. While I was hurrying home to think in peace about all that Morck had told himself, I had to stop. I held my breath and thought, 'I'm just imagining things because something is creating a constant shadow inside me.'

"Johannes was still standing motionless outside the pharmacist's house. A small window on the second floor with a red curtain shone all by itself. It alone glowed in the dark.

"I went out of my mind. I walked over to him. He didn't see me so I called out to him, quite slowly. He turned his head and looked at me, but it was as if he didn't see me. I carefully took his arm and he came along. I was near tears. 'What's the matter with you, Johannes?' I said. In the light from the streetlight I could see his face. His eyes had that surprised expression they usually had when he was sad about something. His face looked drawn and old. Johannes's nose is so impossible and funny you could weep. In his worried face that night it looked so strange it could have knocked you to your knees. There was something naked about his face, and when I scolded him for standing there for hours getting wet he tried to smile but it was as if his lips were frozen. What could I say, what could I do? There was something about him that I couldn't help him with, so I gave him stupid motherly advice and told him to drink something warm and get warmed up when he got home. But I was so desperate I almost didn't have the breath with which to speak.

"He said I could come along and warm him. He grabbed my arm. I could feel a delicate shaking in his arm as it held me like steel. It clung to me.

"Well. Of course, I went along. It was an impossible, insane night. He was crazy and a stranger. He squeezed me until I screamed. And he whispered to me, hot, unbelievable words. I was what he wanted me to be. I was a tart. Yes. There's a whore in almost every woman.

"He kissed me blindly afterwards. He said I must come every single evening. I must come and stay with him. He growled and bit my shoulder until it bled. He kissed my mouth to shreds.

"The air glittered with birdsong as I left. It was almost completely light.

"And still I felt desire and the feverish happiness over being together every night.

"But a heavy darkness weighed down and sank into my very depths. Because I was thinking, 'Johannes is very, very unhappy.' "

"Was every human being doomed to being unhappy in their own lonely world? I thought until I was befuddled and slow. Mrs. Nilsen told me off about the way I was cleaning the rooms. And she was right. I cheated when I could and hated the work more and more. Morck couldn't have more sincerely hated his work as a cafe musician than I hated my work. He had told me about that time when he was playing the sleaziest kind of music in a cafe with red lights, for a pitiful pay. He dreamed of becoming a great pianist and was half starving so he could pay by the hour to practice his études in a piano warehouse. That's where he practiced himself into 'the happy wrath," as he called it, which drove him with passionate zeal into working to better the lot of musicians. He was carried away by that work. He became an embittered fighter for the cause of those who toil in this world. His girl friend worked in the kitchen at the same cafe and she grabbed her coat and quit when he was fired because of being an agitator. She got a job in a laundry. She worked herself to the bone doing overtime and cleaning offices in the mornings. She supported them both until he started getting some piano students. Oh no, it was horrible. I'll tell you about it later.

"Morck was an unhappy person. I was unhappy. Johannes was unhappy. And nobody could help each other.

"At first I didn't want to go to Johannes's the next evening. I thought he probably hadn't meant it that much. But I couldn't let it be. I imagined that Johannes was unhappy. I had to go to him, just to see him. His eyes were so tender when he saw me, you can't imagine, and I think he was glad I'd come, at first. When we entered the living room he wasn't quite so pleased any more. He said he had a headache. That was all right. He was tired and out of sorts. I wasn't really disappointed. All I really wanted was to be in his place, knowing it was just the two of us in his living room. I asked for a cigarette. Then I wanted to leave. He said, 'Oh, really, that too.' He made a remark about my having been drinking wine the night before. He wasn't angry; there was just something ominous in his voice. No, not jealousy, but, but disdain, sort of. He said he didn't want to ask me where I'd been, who I'd been with, late at night. I smoked then. I couldn't say anything. But I finally got up to go and I said I'd been with a man who was unhappy and that I'd drunk wine with him. Nothing more. And I asked if he believed me.

"He was more than happy to believe me. He shrugged his shoulders, it was my business. Unhappy? Who the hell was anything else?

"We sat there for a while and I found out that people were talking about me and this organist. My drinking was a known fact; I'd already established that up at The Mine last summer. You could believe anything about the organist, Morck. There had been talk about getting him fired from his job; he was an annoyance to church sounds. He played secular music in God's house at night. Johannes really wasn't religious—he gladly admitted that—but he agreed that such an organist was somewhat scandalous for the town. In addition, he had heard a few things about Morck, about his earlier life, and if it was true the man should have been fired long ago. Everybody knew about his drinking, but about his being a communist and being run out of his job at a cafe very few people knew. Johannes had found out by chance. You couldn't very well have a damned thing like that participating in sermons.

"I was looking at him, at my JOHANNES, and became profoundly sad. Not for my own sake or for Morck's, but for Johannes's. They'd gotten him to where they wanted him, to be the way you had to be in that town. He was accepted by decent company. He played cards with both the pharmacist and the veterinarian.

"What about Morck? He'd come to this town to escape from the bottle. He'd wanted to submit himself to the middle-class values of a small town and become the church organist and attempt to become a respectable human being anyway and get married and have children. He walked right into the trap. The town could not stomach a man like Morck. He was an artist and different. He had one blue and one brown eye and was therefore further capable of just about anything.

"If there is one place in the world that will make you an alcoholic, it's our town.

"When I got up to leave he said, 'Don't look so sad. I'm a little out of sorts today. Come back another time.'

"I brightened up. I said, 'When?'

"He thought about it and mentioned a day, a few days later. And I was happy, kissed his mouth and both his hands."

She stopped. She closed her eyes with a tired expression. I got up and turned out the lights. It was raining outside, a dense and soundless rain.

140

The streets were shiny. It had become quiet. It was that time of the morning when it gets quiet again after the day has first started to stir. It's as if the morning stops to listen for a while. I sat down again and lit a cigarette.
She opened her eyes and looked at me without changing position.

"Well, I was walking around being pretty happy during those days, thinking everything would be all right. In fact, he had a lot to teach me and I would surely find the part of him that was right. I thought I could probably make him understand what made the organist be the way he was, that which raised him above everybody else in town, in his misery. Yes, I was as happy as I could expect to be. On the evening I was going to see him I made up my mind to do everything in my power to put him in a good mood. He was sad about something that would probably take time to heal, but then everything would be fine between us. I looked out and saw his window while I was getting dressed up to go see him, and I blew a kiss toward his window. I hummed and brushed my hair, but when I looked that way again the light was suddenly turned off. I stood there with the hairbrush in my hand, 'Could this be right?' I stared and stared, hoping I'd seen wrong. But it was dark at Johannes's.

"Well, if only I hadn't been so happy a moment earlier. You should never be so happy. I was probably making much too much out of this. He'd probably gone to bed. He was probably waiting for me and wanted to sleep a little first. That's probably the way things were. I put on my clothes. But I couldn't find my happiness again. There was some kind of reluctance in me as I walked up to his place. I thought there was probably something painful about to happen again, I was probably about to be in pain again.

"It was locked. The basement door leading to the kitchen was locked. But he was expecting me. I tried to chase my fear away. It had to be forgetfulness. Maybe he'd gone on an errand, to talk to someone, something like that. I'd never seen anything so dark as those windows. The house was completely dead. I walked home an hour later, tired and feeling hopeless.

"Far into the morning a light went on at Johannes's. A little while later it went out. I went to bed then with all my clothes on.

"Oh, those days. My body felt as if it had been through a meat grinder from lack of sleep. Johannes was in my thoughts all the time, poisoning me completely. Any kind of work was torture, and so was idleness. I had to force myself to stay home when there was a light on at his place. I was in a cold sweat and my stomach was upset.

"He dropped in on the shop. He looked at me tentatively, looking pale and worn. But there was spring sunshine in his eyes. I couldn't speak a word to him because my hands shook so and my lips shook when I tried to smile. I found something to do among the shelves and felt his glance like a sweet pain through my whole body. There were other people in the shop and I almost wished he'd leave before the others, but he waited. When we were alone he said I looked bad, like I needed to get away for a while to take care of myself and rest. I grabbed hold of it, drank deeply of the fact that he cared about me and noticed that I didn't look good. I gathered in the fact that he had also said we should go away together. I gathered up happiness from this and that and thought, 'Everything will be well as soon as I am better balanced and not so touchy about little things. He probably has his difficulties and forgets an appointment from time to time, but that will pass and we'll have a lot of good times together.'

"As he left he bought two packs of fine Dutch cigarettes of an expensive kind he never used to smoke. He gave one of them to me. Well, I got quite embarrassed and shy with pleasure. It was the first time he'd given me anything, given me a little gift.

"And you know, I really did manage to pull myself together into some kind of balance. I managed to fall asleep at night, and I managed to chase away the kinds of thoughts that bothered the living daylights out of me. I forced myself to eat properly and thought to myself that when I was feeling stronger everything else would be better too. I bought cod liver oil and concentrated on becoming healthy and pretty . . . for Johannes. Johannes, Johannes, Johannes!

"Hoping helped. There were moments when I felt enormously happy at managing the situation, at overcoming the situation. I didn't understand that this presumptuousness was itself an expression of weakness."

"One day I walked up toward The Mine with some eggs for my mother and a paper cone full of licorice sticks and sugar candy for my brother, a precious gift for a cheerless toiler of fourteen. There was a veil of green across all the hills. It was cloudy with the kind of silver gray clouds that make the sunshine blind and white; it cut coldly into your eyes. The blue rifts in the cloud cover were the kind of intense blue that warns of wet weather. It was good and muddy on the country road and I was walking along, humming. The air was full of promises. My nose was cold and I could feel full spring coming on. My blood sort of floated in my veins and made my body dizzy with some vague notion about spring and summer lying in wait somewhere behind that penetrating wind, and about all of life's delights waiting somewhere for someone who'd had a bad time and was capable of receiving them. If I was thinking at all, this was the thought I was probably having.

"Then I saw Johannes. I suddenly saw only Johannes. He was carrying something. The whole thing was too unbelievable to grasp all at once; it could have been a sack or a bicycle. I was seeing Johannes with eyes that popped out of my head. There he suddenly was at a turn in the road. Something made me feel as if a heavy rock had been thrown at my stomach. My first conscious thought was to get going. 'Just walk and look as if nothing is happening and don't stop and don't collapse.' So I walked on heedlessly, maybe a little faster, not a drop of blood left in my brain or my body; I just walked on. Someone had thrown a rock at my diaphragm.

"He was walking with a woman, close together. Their arms were linked and Johannes's eyes shone. My lips were tingling with numbness. The skin on my scalp shrank.

"To tell you the truth, I don't remember another thing about that trip to The Mine. I couldn't tell you, if my life depended on it, how I got home. But I do remember that on the following morning there was a bag with two eggs and a miserable paper cone full of goodies on my dresser. Not until then did I cry, and the paper cone did it. The strangest things set you off sometimes.

"What happened later on that evening seems to me utterly ludicrous. But it couldn't have happened any other way. From the way I've turned out since, you'd think it natural that I thought too much, that I took it all too seriously back then.

"But it couldn't have happened otherwise. I know I'm right when I say I felt as if what happened that evening threw me into an abyss. Well, that night I went to bed with someone named Mohn, a traveling salesman at the hotel. It isn't at all the first one who takes the ground out from under a woman's feet.

"It's the second one. Number two is the beginning. It's the first happenstance that constitutes a woman's fall, as they say.

Morning had come alive with a vengeance. Trucks, bicycles. On the staircase you could hear the singing noise of a waterbucket being moved, and the sputtering of someone scrubbing the stairs. A vacuum cleaner was started up upstairs. A streetcar screamed down the tracks.

"Well, dammit. I don't remember how it happened. How it started, I mean. It was like waking up after you've fainted. I was standing in my room, trying to light the lamp with limp, powerless hands. I was beginning to ache inside. One single hurricanelike thought was running through me: 'I can't stand it.' Someone knocked on the door. I hadn't locked it. I was standing there holding my breath and with a fluttering heart waiting for a miracle to happen, that it would be Johannes arriving. It was Mohn. He said, 'Why in the name of heaven didn't you say hello to me just now?' But I couldn't remember having met him and not saying hello. I stood there unable to move, knocked out by the fact that it wasn't Johannes, never, never again. I felt an angry nausea because Mohn took the lamp away from me and wanted it to be dark and embraced me. He must have noticed how unwilling I was. He let go of me and lit the lamp for me. The sea was roaring maliciously down at the tideline. And Mohn looked honestly surprised when he saw my face in the lamplight. At first he wanted to touch me again, I think it was out of helpless sympathy, but I said, 'Go, go.'

"But when he opened the door and I saw his back, I could hear the sea and could hear that it and loneliness would not wish me well. I called out, 'Don't leave me.' I was seasick with pain.

"Of what he said I can only remember his mentioning the words 'a glass of wine.' I sucked in that word 'wine.' Wine, lots of wine, no thinking, just drinking.

"Well, I made myself hurry to dress and wash up. I fixed myself up in order to be a little bit nice to Mohn. He'd gone off to arrange things in the living room, where we'd agreed to sit after I, with utmost irritability, had refused his room.

"He had wound something red around the lamp in the living room. I didn't like it, but the only thing I saw was the wine bottle and the glasses he'd provided. He'd been in the kitchen and found a little jam pot for holding the cigarettes and he'd put little place cards of the kind he sold at our seats, with our names carefully inscribed. Oh, he really wanted to make it nice for me and comfort me as best he could. He looked at me expectantly and sort of didn't dare smile. Well, you know, I had to smile myself, because I really wanted to cry my eyes out because he was so nice to me.

"Yes, wine's a strange thing. If your sorrows have taken all the blood out of your body, wine will bring it back. You can feel it begin to glow with pleasure. And your head gets lighter, your thoughts lighter; a drop of joy that spreads the warmth of the wine through your body may arrive. Cold waves of pain went through me, but I hurried to drink them away until my mind was quite dull.

"From far away, sort of, I could hear myself sitting there getting talkative. I was sitting on the couch with my head resting on Mohn's arm, and I didn't mind. What did I talk about?

"Oh, I was spinning a tale about a man I knew. I was philosophizing about the fact that an artist was such a slave to his art that he could betray his morals, could betray what he had fought for and betray his girl friend in a vile way because of an opportunity to cultivate his music.

"Mohn was playing with my hair. He said, 'No, let's drink a toast.'

"I said, 'It must be horrible for him to think about. All for that kind of a woman, one of those who thrives on the hard work of others. And old. Much older than him. She was used to buying whatever she wanted and she bought him. He got an education and he got a wonderful grand piano.'

"Mohn said he liked Hawaiian music. Hawaiian music in the moonlight was the best. I said I couldn't stop thinking about that girl, the girl he left. She died while he was in Germany. A big illegal abortion scandal was uncovered because she died after such an operation. Mohn said, 'Let's talk about something nicer.' He was playing with my hair. But I'd gotten sentimental. I said, 'His first concert had to be cancelled. Because he'd suddenly taken to drinking himself into oblivion. The vilest of all was what he'd been feeling all along, that he'd let himself be bought with the gold that those other poor cafe musicians were cheated out of. Yes, isn't it terrible?'

"And Mohn answered that he thought that was terrible indeed, but we should drink a toast.

"So we drank. I cried a little because he didn't want to listen to me. When he started to kiss my throat I didn't think that was so bad, but I'd had to drink a lot to like it. I laughed and hummed and kept reality feverishly at a distance. As soon as Mohn left for a moment it all came crashing down on me as if I hadn't had a drop to drink. While I was sitting here getting drunk with a strange man, Johannes was sleeping with another woman. It was all so heartbreakingly clear to me I threw myself down on the couch with abject weeping.

"Mohn quieted my tears with kisses and caresses. But mostly with port. I let myself be anesthetized. I emptied glass after glass and let myself tumble into a dance of indifference. Well, I managed to convince myself that now I would be through with Johannes; now I would burn all my bridges. Cheers! I accepted as something good and right all that cheap red light and Mohn's indiscreet caresses and the port drunk. I let myself be carried along without doing a thing to save myself.

146

"When we snuck into his room and I was holding his hand, I thought Mohn was nice and handsome and that I was certainly quite in love with him. He complained about my grip on his hand. There were nailmarks on it."

She stopped and swallowed. She wiped her forehead. I noticed that her face was gray. She moistened her lips, held out her glass, and looked questioningly at me. I poured it full with an unsteady hand. She drank it greedily. Then she continued in a voice that had lost all its timbre. It was quite colorless.

"But in the morning when I woke up after a short sleep in my own bed in a whirlwind of dreams and the gray light of day washed over me, I couldn't move. There was a hurricane of despair inside me. There was a pool of hideousness left. Well, well. Maybe it was just a small thing. But every time I closed my eyes I could see Mohn, who'd let go of me as soon as it was over and hurried to the sink, where he washed in a hurry. I didn't understand it at first. To tell you the truth, I didn't understand the meaning of what he was doing at the sink, only that it filled me with hopeless shame.

"Mohn, poor sinner, couldn't comprehend my hateful coldness toward him after that."

"So then we had our spring. It came roaring over us with foaming birches along blue ponds and glittering gold from the throats of birds rejoicing throughout the woods.

"Like a thief I snuck to and from work. My room became like a prison I could not escape from because the spring outside wanted nothing to do with me. Such a chamber, such a room can become a pest-ridden hole from housing a person's lonely torments. They take up their places in the walls and ceiling and all the objects and greet you with scorn every time you open the door to such a room. I've never hated anything so profoundly as that room and that bed. In that bed lay all the painful thoughts from sleepless nights. Everything painful stays on in such a bed and makes its home there and cannot be driven out.

"Listen here, I was completely crazy. Svanhild was her name, the daughter of the pharmacist in town. She was pretty, very pretty. I'd seen her often. For a while there was talk that she and Johannes were engaged. That quieted down and for a time I heard that she was about to make a good match with a fellow from the capital. She traveled a lot. I felt safe about her after a while. She looked pretty and proper. I sometimes liked her with something close to a perverse passion. Well, listen to this, this is desperate and strange, but jealousy is something peculiar. And this spring I was out of my mind. I don't know what else to say. Now that I knew, yes, I mean *knew* everything, down to the last detail, now, I began to look at her. Fearfully at first, yes, scared to death. Her features burned into my mind when I was alone in my room. They were alive and relentlessly close when I couldn't sleep. As if they were Johannes himself. Her face mingled with his until I was ready to scream. Then up and to the window to see if there was a light on behind his curtains at night. Well, I sought some kind of peace from the possibility that it would be dark at his place, from his sleeping and being alone. Sometimes I could fool myself into some sort of feeling of exhausted happiness this way. Freedom from pain. Do you think I would leave myself alone and let it go at that? Oh, no. If his place was dark some evening, the thought would occur to me that maybe he was at her place. Well, it was sheer craziness, but I was driven and forced to go down to the pharmacist's house to convince myself that her place was dark too, so that I could go to sleep. What did I want to accomplish? It couldn't be anything besides driving myself out of my mind. Which I did. On the first night of letting myself be tortured by this thought and this misplaced hope, her place was all lit up, no curtain. Then I thought, 'She's alone.' Otherwise the curtain would have been drawn. And I should have hurried home. I later regretted not having hurried to get home. But I stayed there. To make quite sure. Then the curtain was closed, the red curtain. For one piercing, steely second I watched it being closed. Johannes was closing it.

"There I stood like a pillar of salt. In a storm of sheer pain. While the spring night smelled fragrant, hummed and whispered its carelessness into my ear.

"I didn't want to know, but I was forced to know and I knew every time. I was with them in bed. They killed me with each one of their embraces. And my chamber shared all this maddening pain with me. It came to live there. If I managed to sleep for a couple of hours on any given night, I'd wake at dawn, my thoughts wreaking havoc with me. During this whole year with Johannes, with one thing happening after the other, a nagging stumbling block had appeared which told me that he'd lied to me quite often, that Svanhild had been there the whole time. Both Svanhild and I had been there the whole time, but mainly for him it had been Svanhild. The sea outside heard my thoughts and roared them back at me. It stirred like an eggbeater in my open wounds. It was aware but without a trace of compassion.

"I looked frightful. Thin and awful. Hopelessly ugly. Everyone I looked at was happy and pretty. There was real warmth in the sunshine now and the young girls had gotten out their summer dresses. I hid my long, skinny body in my worn winter coat, which was too warm, but in which I was cold anyway.

"One night I couldn't take it any more. I quite simply wanted to get drunk in order to rest in drunkenness and oblivion for a whole night. Then I'd try to pull myself together. I knocked on Morck's door, worried that he wouldn't have anything to drink in the house.

"He had some gin. He grabbed both my arms when I came inside and without a word he looked at me under the light. He let go and found the bottle. 'Right,' he said.

"The gin was much too strong for me. The air in his room was dense and nauseating. I wanted to force myself to drink; everything would be better when the liquor started working. But it just immediately rushed around in my head and I got unbearably nauseous. I tried to get up. Morck grabbed hold of me, but I yelled, 'Go away!'

"Then it happened. Before I knew it I was throwing up with such force that my whole body heaved with convulsions. I thought, 'That's what I get for not eating. Starting tomorrow I'll force myself to eat.'

"I sat down dejectedly and just looked dully at Morck, who found a bucket and a rag and started cleaning up after me. He said, 'The place needed a cleaning, good thing you decided to do this.' I was attacked by a soothing fatigue as he was busying himself with cleaning up. I fell asleep in the chair. I woke up only once while he was lifting me up and putting me down on his bed. He covered me up real well and sat down on a chair next to the bed, watching over me with one blue and one brown eye.

"When I woke up the morning sun was coloring everything in the room red and Morck was sitting there in the same position, but the bottle on the table was almost empty and Morck's face looked sort of erased, although his eyes were fastened on me still. It felt good not to be in my own evil room and in my own evil bed. I told Morck that if I'd had a small amount of money I would leave town. Morck said, 'Just you sleep,' and I sank down into a nice cool drowsiness and fell asleep. Far into the day Morck woke me up with warm milk and thick slices of bread that I ate down to the last crumb. As I walked home I felt in better spirits than I had for a long time and I didn't even bat an eye telling Mrs. Nilsen I'd spent the night at my mother's up at The Mine.

"Morck had opened up a hope in me, a pale and frightened little hope. Before I left he'd said that if it was the last thing he did on this earth, he wanted to help me so that I'd at least have a chance in life. Just to have someone wanting to help, someone who understood how difficult it was to be me and who wanted to help, made me have to cry a little before I went to the store, you know.

"Oh, how he really tried to help me later. And it was the last thing he did on this earth, that's true. He had wanted to give me everything, but there wasn't a stitch left when all his debts had been settled. I was in a clinic when it happened, but I cried for joy, nevertheless."

She'd put her fingers to her mouth and was kissing them a little while looking straight ahead with a distant tenderness in her eyes.

"It was strange, you know, but I sort of felt relieved when Johannes and Svanhild took out their wedding announcement. There had been no official engagement but they announced their wedding anyway. He wasn't waiting to finish his education, after all. Johannes was getting married without feeling he could afford it. He didn't show up at the shop during this period and I was happy about that. I'd begun to be able to eat again. If I forgot to, I would be struck by a ravenous hunger.

"One day I'd forgotten to eat dinner. I was in the shop arranging some magazines I'd picked up at the post office. At first I felt hungry. Sudden, demanding hunger. I nabbed a banana and went into the back room to wolf it down. But I had to sit down in there. I thought it would probably pass quickly; I just had to quit thinking about whether or not there was a light on at Johannes's at night. A cold trickle ran down my face. My forehead was damp and a whole telephone pole began singing inside my head. Little black balls danced around and around in my brain, nausea grabbed my throat, and then I blacked out.

"Well, I was gone for a year or so, living a storm of madness and strange happenings. Then the telephone pole sang in my brain again and I woke up when two men lifted me off the chair and laid me flat on the floor. It had just lasted for a moment. They'd heard me hit the table and whimper when they came in. They sent for Madsen and wanted to send me home, but I was recovering and didn't want to go home. Madsen wouldn't give in. He said he wouldn't subtract a cent from my pay. I was to go home and rest. He'd rather have me gone for a few hours to get some rest than have me be as slow as I'd been lately.

"So I went. But I didn't want to go home at any price. I was really feeling pretty good right then. Fainting had sort of lightened up my head. The air was clean and mild. The light veil of clouds lent a melancholy note to the sun's perpetual spring smile.

"It was that time of the afternoon when children are out playing their hardest. The narrow streets reverberated with the song of children's laughter, screams, and raucous voices. I was watching some little girls playing hopscotch. They were quarreling terribly over whether or not the line had been stepped on, and I discovered I could smile. That smile gave birth to hope.

"If you can smile today, maybe you can laugh tomorrow, and before you know it you'll be young again. Well, that's probably the way I was thinking. I went to the cafe and stood myself to a roll with sausage and a glass of milk and I enjoyed the fresh roll with real country butter. I was in the cafe where Johannes and I had made plans to travel once. It stung when I remembered it, but I forced myself to think about it and told myself I would stand thinking about everything that had happened. 'You're going to learn to remember everything without it knocking you to your knees.' That way I would become stronger after a while.

"I bought a package of nice rolls with cold cuts on them as I left. I wanted to take a trip up to The Mine. It had been a long time since the last time I went. I went into a store and bought fifty øres worth of chocolate.

"The cloud cover had been erased once again and the sun shone behind the treetops. It followed me as I walked. It danced along in the treetops in front of me. It hid here and there behind the scattered firs on top of the hill and squirted explosions of light in my eyes when it reappeared. I discovered the world again. I was still alive and dared enjoy it.

"A bird whistled a sorrowful question at me. It whistled the note upward, an accurate question mark of a note. I stopped and answered. I whistled the same note downward, "So, now you know, little friend." Imagine, it took to the conversation with delight. It hurried to repeat my answer; it was unbelievable. Then we both listened for a while and then it tried again, with my note. And I answered with the questioning note and here it came again from the treetops, rejoicing with the sense of company. We went on like this for a while until I definitely had to open the package and eat a roll. I was eating a fresh sausage sandwich and listening, chewing and listening. My little friend in the tree tried both questions and answers when I was quiet and finally it gave up. It swayed on the branch of the fir tree for a moment; then it was gone. I sighed and wrapped the paper carefully around the leftover sandwiches. Yes, life was full of pleasures that were just waiting for me to come to my senses. Just the fact that fresh sausage sandwiches once again had importance and meaning about them was good. My palate responding was good.

"Well, that's the way I was feeling life coming back, like a person convalescing after a huge illness. That's the way it is. We don't die from love.

"As I approached The Mine I discovered that I was walking in a careful circle to avoid the place where my mother lived. With a sweet little jolt I knew where I wanted to go. I wanted to see my sister. Or her little boy, rather.

"He'd become a big boy of about six months. He was sitting up in bed like a grown man, chewing his hands and itching his gums. He was drooling mightily and had a sore chin, but his cheeks were red and newly washed and his hair smelled of fine soap. He was fretting a little, waiting for his food. When he saw the plate he laughed angrily and impatiently.

"There was something I wanted to tell you about this, but now I've forgotten. I can only remember about my sister's baby boy now. I was allowed to feed him. When he started being full and was fooling around, I pretended to put the spoon in my own mouth. He opened his own wide with fury. You know, there was something very important I wanted to tell you, but his bib smelled of sour milk and his neck of warm infant. I was pretending to bite his neck with my lips until he screamed with laughter.

"My brother-in-law wasn't at home. Oh, now I remember. I wanted to tell you about the buildings, those new workers' housing complexes that the factory had had built. There was built-in water and electricity. Not many people had electricity yet, back then. My sister was discontent anyway. She moaned and complained. Mostly about Amund. And the apartment . . . it was all right with lights going on at the touch of a button and water running in the sink at the turn of a tap, but. Nothing was painted, there was just bare wood that would get ugly unless she scrubbed it all the time. She'd just been terribly sick, she was still sick. And Amund begrudged her everything. He'd gotten her pregnant almost as soon as they were married. Fortunately, she knew how to take care of that but she'd been sick afterwards, very sick. If she had to go through that one more time, she'd die. But she'd rather die than have more children, the way Amund was. He carried on about her having bought just a flower-patterned coverlet for the crib and swore when she said she needed her shoes resoled. Well, I didn't know what to say, you know. I tried to change the subject and said she looked good, even though I didn't mean it at all because she'd turned old under the eyes and had sunken temples. She got angry then. She got quite unbalanced and said she'd have me know she was ill, felt awful, and could hardly drag herself around, and if I wanted to see for myself . . . Well, shamelessly, as only a woman can be with another woman, she lifted her dress and showed me her underwear. I laid down on the bed and didn't want to see any more, and then she changed the subject and asked if I was feeling bad. I mumbled something about not being able to stand the sight of blood. Well, well, I lived my carefree life of egotism and fainted at the sight of a drop of blood. I should only know, I should know what kind of torture a poor working man's wife had to go through if she wanted to avoid even more misery.

"Amund was not among those who were the worst paid. He was a skilled machinist with a good salary from the machine shop at The Mine. At home they'd rather thought she'd done well to get him. I mentioned to her that our father hadn't made as much as Amund did.

"But then there was the rent. Almost a whole week's wages went just for rent and then there was the expensive electricity; they could keep their electricity so far as she was concerned, she'd rather live in those awful barracks on The Hill and carry water; she was used to that. She'd rather be able to afford a little pleasure, some good food and such, and avoid all that scolding about using too much of this or that because they couldn't make ends meet.

"Oh, how she talked. I was no longer paying attention. I was thinking about her somehow having gotten rid of a fetus, voluntarily giving up the experience of another baby boy. The experience that could be the most wonderful one for a woman, just like that time when she held her newborn boy to her breast.

"My thoughts were in a strange state that evening when I walked back down to town. It was such a beautiful evening, opalescent from the moonlight and there were clouds scurrying. Why? Why? Everything I thought about ended in an omnipresent 'Why?' I followed the thread of thoughts far enough to find some sort of an answer. I could dimly see that all the threads came together like in a spider's web and that all the things I was thinking about hung together some way or other.

"When you see women who are meant to have babies and who like having children commit secret, bloody crimes against their bodies to avoid having them, you know there is something wrong somewhere. Unless they're completely crazy. In this case you're not talking about amoral and frivolous people but about those who are married and all right.

"Take my sister, for example. If it hadn't been for the money matter and such, she would have had that baby, and had it with pleasure. She was afraid of poverty. All of them up at The Mine are afraid of poverty, and more children means more poverty. There she was with a good place to live—a nice, modern place to live that the factory had built for its workers. And that was nice of the factory, right? The factory has to charge a lot for the rent, because nobody can expect the factory to do things like that for free. What happens is that babies who could have been born into such a nice place to live have to be gotten rid of. They are only allowed to be born into the worst places to live.

"So these nice places become disasters, rather than the opposite. The way I looked at it, the factory had committed that bloody crime against my sister. Here you have one thread in the spiderweb intersecting another. The factory, who is the factory? Is it the workers and the machinery and the cleaning facility and the elevator system and the railroad and the silica-rich earth and the mountain? That's not something you can call responsible for child murder. Those who own the factory are people who live abroad. It isn't even a man, one particular man you can go to and tell this and that. It's stocks and such, and you can't talk to those. They're supposed to make profits. These foreigners don't invest their money in Norwegian factories in order to improve the living conditions of Norwegian workers but in order to have their money multiply.

"I tried to tell my sister some of this, but she didn't want to listen. She said, 'Don't start in with politics!' She'd had more than enough politics from listening to Amund. She was much too tired to get involved in that kind of men's talk and she'd had enough of his spending nearly all his free time going to meetings and the like, married man that he was.

"Politics? I didn't even know back then that this was politics. It gave me lots to ponder that was too difficult for me. I thought it was just some sort of mathematics, a black kind of mathematics that they'd forgotten to teach us in high school. We certainly had more of a need to know about politics, something real, than we did about equations and such. And as I walked home in the opalescent moon darkness and was beginning to hear the sea whispering when I got closer to town, I made up my mind to bring newspapers home from the store and to read all sorts of papers just to see if there was something that could make all my loose threads come together.

"Well, you know, I was so preoccupied by all this that I walked through that town which had become sort of poisoned by all my bad memories and where every rock, every tree, every house had seen my misery and knew about all my humiliations, and I didn't remember any of this until I smelled the sea down in the alley that led to Mrs. Nilsen's hotel. As you got close to my lodgings you felt as though someone was holding a fresh mussel shell under your nose, and I thought everything would have to be just the way it was. I felt tied to the place and loved it in a way. My room was the same. As soon as I came inside, darkness and loneliness swept over my mind and it came to me that Johannes was . . . well, there was a light on behind his curtains. What had happened was that I felt strong enough to bear the pain. That was something new, something that pointed to the strength in me, saying, 'There's something in store for you.' Well, you know, it all gathered together into some of what I had been feeling that night in church. I made up my mind that I had to make Morck play for me again. In return, I'd ask to clean and fix up his room a few days a week. He was my only friend.

"Lots of things were stirring in me during those days. I remember those days, minute by minute. Everything about Johannes was still there; it wasn't over, but I carried it the way you carry a heavy burden, gritting your teeth and telling yourself you will make it to the top of the hill. I could feel that there was an end in sight somewhere. If only I could stand it and not give up and starve myself and get sick, a time would come when I could lay down my burden and see the view from the top of the hill.

"I slept well that night. But I woke up very, very early with some disturbance I couldn't get hold of. Something foreboding. It felt as if I'd forgotten something. I had to fight against it. I fought against something invisible and slippery. I searched through everything I'd thought about the day before and found it but couldn't get ahold of it. With the first crow of a rooster in a chicken house far away, I got up and got dressed. It was still dead and quiet in the streets outside, but in the gardens all around there was an eager business of birds. Far up on the hill there was a song sparkling on the air like a glittering wellspring of joy. It was flung up into the air, where it burst into thousands of golden drops that fluttered across space. The little singer up in the tree sounded as if he was about to burst with happiness. I was standing right up against a fence, letting all this joy into my wounds and scratches until it burned, and thought I had to learn to endure until I'd learned to be happy.

"Maybe that was a stupid, foolish thought, but it felt as

though it was wisely and strongly thought. I hung on to the fence post and gained courage that way. Even then there was something scratching at me about having forgotten something. Then I saw someone sneaking hurriedly along the garden walls in the upper streets and I recognized her from her raven black hair. I was watching Svanhild tiptoeing home from my Johannes's place. I clenched my teeth until they hurt and gripped the fence post until the wood cut into my hand and thought hard as could be that here it was, here was that painful thing that had been buried so obscurely in me. Now I could accept the pain and become calm once again. Well, the pain was clear enough. I'd tiptoed that way from his place on many a morning. I let the wave wash through me like boiling sea spray. I relived the hot exhaustion from Johannes's embrace, the small painful happiness that carried with it a longing for the next time. And here I was, the world's loneliest girl in a glittering spring morning, while his woman hurried home right under my eyes, warm and happy. I stood there, complaining a little and accepting the pain. I thought, 'It'll pass. It'll pass. It has to pass sometime.' Tears were in my eyes from the pain. But something fantastic had happened. Remember that I was only eighteen years old; that's not very old. Trembling seizures of bitter desire were writhing in me, along with a terrible pain wracking my body. But I didn't collapse, nor did I run away. I didn't give in. This is what had happened: I'd started to fight. My consciousness was at work. I was looking at the inferno with hard open eyes. This, you see, was like having received a gift. A bitter gift, a heavy, demanding, wearisome gift, but a gift nonetheless. It felt like the strength of passion; hard, gray passion, but not without its own bitter pleasure. Listen here, do you understand any of this? I am less scared when I know you've understood what I want you to. Yes, I'm afraid. I don't know, but sometimes that gray fear grabs me and drives me like a leaf before the wind. Afraid? No, not afraid, I'm not afraid. Not any more."

Her hands had become restless. She was fiddling with her suitcase. She opened it and dug out a little box. Her hands played with it a little, opened and closed it. Then she quickly put it back in the suitcase, which she closed with a bang and placed back down on the floor.

"Well, what was I talking about? Now I know, it was about the time the organist created a scandal in church. Was that it? I'm all messed up, I'm mixing everything up. When these pains start I can't think. But I have to, I have to tell you all this, because I'm in a hurry. What time is it now? I'm getting distracted, you see, by something far back that I haven't told you. I thought it wasn't important. It concerns Johannes and is about his bad start. He too had a chain to drag along through life, I'll tell you. It's not romantic, it's about money. He had a good education. He'd become a teacher, but he was poorer than a mine worker. Oh, I've heard a lot of good-luck stories in my life, about people starting out with two empty hands and who, through diligence and being careful and purposeful, etcetera, etcetera. Someone I knew, his name was Carl, he was that way. He had lots of money in the bank and a fish market that made him rich. I was even married to him for two years. Did I tell you I was married once? He was what you call self-made. But I know that whoever is self-made and manages to become wealthy has to be equipped with a big lack of scruples or be pretty audacious, (aside from having diligence and ability). It's no accident that audacity is called a gift of God.

"Oh boy, oh boy, what a mess I'm making. It's only Johannes playing tricks on me now. A man who starts out with a debt is like the man in the legend—well, I don't remember his name. I'm aching with craziness right now, and I'm cold because death has a cold breath. The one in the legend, the one who struggles with the heavy rock, who every time he gets it in place sees it roll back down. Oh, God, it's impossible to think straight, but wasn't that the way it was? And Johannes carries his burdens so quietly; he always treads quietly, Johannes does.

"What about that spring morning I was telling you about? I remember it all now—yes, good God, it's all coming alive. I suffered on behalf of Johannes then and discovered that I could watch my suffering with open eyes without collapsing. I told

160

myself that now I would be through with Johannes. How many times in my life have I been finally through with Johannes?

"I'll never be through with Johannes.

"One morning many years ago I went for a walk. I tore myself away from a fence where I had nearly become rooted with pain, a pain that many people have experienced on spring mornings up through the ages. I waded through a violent shower of birdsong in the young forest and experienced a hard pleasure from knowing there was strength hidden in my own consciousness, in my thirst for knowledge, in my sense of being a human being in a world full of human beings toiling in their chains."

"I had to talk to someone. I longed for day and for people to come out of their houses so that I could see them and say hello to them quite silently, by myself. It was like a promise.

"Working people were going to the factory as I walked home. There was smoke from the chimneys, and voices echoed in the quiet streets along with heavy workboot footsteps. The factory manager's summer estate sat with closed shutters blindly staring across the bay toward the town. There it sat in the morning sun like the palace of Sleeping Beauty. No one lived there except the groundskeeper, who made sure no one broke into the wine cellar or the weapons collection or the antiques collection and all the beautiful things in there, which no one enjoyed except for a few weeks during the summer. No one other than the groundskeeper, Tellefsen and his wife, that is. They had a little house to themselves and a nice life and a nice salary for looking after it all.

"Yes, it was a fine morning. But then there was this thing, this feeling that I'd forgotten something. Something I could not remember. It was like hearing quick footsteps behind you, but every time I'd turn to look there was nothing there.

"In the evening I bought a whole bunch of newspapers, two apples, and a bag of wheat rolls to take home. I wanted to have a nice time.

"I munched on an apple and read about strikes at the docks and that the socialists were killing the country's economic life and laying it waste. There was something about public-spirited people, a group of stout, brave young men who defied the rabble at the docks. They weren't above anyone; they loaded and un-loaded like ordinary workers in order to save Norway's commercial life. There was a cheerful little article with a funny drawing alongside about how the striking workers could calmly take a hike or sun themselves on park benches because the Vikings weren't dead yet. And the workers were welcome to get drunk on weekdays even; they were being supported by Moscow and had no problems.

"Yes, that's what it said and I munched down both the apple core and the stem.

"I knew what a strike meant for the workers. My father had participated in a strike at The Mine a few years earlier. That winter we went into the forest to gather dead branches for fire-wood for the stove and there was little food to be bought with the few kroner the association paid out in strike support. Worst of all were my mother's tears and harping. She said, 'Politics will make us starve to death. You ought to be grateful you have a job and thank God you're not unemployed.' We'd been through that too. She said all of it was instigation and politics and that it was the women who had to pay.

"It was awful at home then. My father was upset and short-tempered. He couldn't stand very much of that harping. He tried to explain to her that this was the workers' fight and the strike his only weapon. If he gave up or failed in this fight he would be betraying the whole working class. There were such scenes that we kids hid. Sometimes my father would leave in anger and come back drunk the next morning. Then it was awful all over, more miserable than ever. My mother said, 'We were doing all right the way things were, we didn't have to starve.' My father said, 'Yes, because workers before us fought we don't have to starve.' And my mother sniffled into her apron and was of the opinion that we should be satisfied then. Then my father said, 'Yes, we. Maybe you, and us right here. There are just five of us, so we're scraping by. But what about the others, those who have five or seven children?' My mother screamed at him about people learning to watch it, about men learning to control them-selves.

"He went out drinking again that night. He got drunk quite often, just like the time before we moved to The Mine, when he was without a job.

"Here was a well-written, reasonable article in a newspaper saying that drunkenness was on the upswing during the strike, and that just proved what kind of rabble it was that wanted to force their wishes through by striking. 'They don't want to work,' it said. 'They're drunken individuals,' it said. There was something about wifebeating, about getting drunk and coming home and beating up their wives. People ought to be aware what kinds of forces were behind the strikes, the dregs of society, the lowest level of the population.

"I ate all the rolls. I almost inhaled them and swallowed them down with milk. I had to talk to Morck. He was the only one I could talk to. There was something specific I had to have ex-plained; maybe this was the constant, indiscernible restlessness I felt.

"Morck was at home. It was early in the evening and he had just gotten up. He was sober and pale. You cannot believe what a handsome man Morck was when he was sober. He shaved for me and was happy that I'd come. I could see that he must have been very beautiful before his teeth decayed and his hair faded. That night we disagreed for the first time. I got a little heated and unfriendly, but it gave me a lot to think about. Listen here."

She had put her suitcase back up on her lap and was rummaging around in it. Her hair was messy and her face shiny. After a moment's thought she took two pills. She found a little handkerchief, which she balled up in her hand. She closed the suitcase and put it down while she continued:

"That evening I told him a little about my life. I told him about having been to the doctor and all that. And I told him about Seamstress Borgny and her boy and about all the little baby boys that were done away with. I told him about my mother and her spiritual and physical decay. I told him that I had discovered that all these things were related and that all the strikes and the unrest among workers were somehow related too. I said, 'It's so awful, it has to be changed. It has to be possible to do something to change it all, and it isn't simple. I understand so little of it, but there must be something wrong somewhere, something awfully wrong.'

"Morck sat on the table supporting one elbow with his hand, smoking a pipe. He was nodding now and then and chewing on the pipe, watching me the whole time. When he finally talked he said something to this effect, 'So, you've experienced that portion of the whole thing called the fetus pogroms.' Fetus pogroms? I didn't know what pogroms were.

"He said, 'Pogroms are most often a symptom. Pogroms are likely to signify the system's death struggle.' Systems. Symptoms. Alien words to me. I just shook my head. He said that life itself would show me the way because I was the kind who carried my emotions in my fingertips and had those rare kind of eyes that were made to see. But I said, 'You have to play for me, that way I'll understand you better.' He just dragged deeply on his pipe and blew thick smoke and said, 'Fetus pogroms is the most disgusting crime committed by the incumbent system. They are the very symptom of cancer.'

"He told me a little bit about cancer. Oh, God, I've come to know what that is. For many years I walked around without any pain. Well, I didn't suspect a thing. Back then I didn't quite understand him when he said that no one made a fuss about these pogroms, only about the accompanying criminality. People wanted to believe that quacks and unhappy women were the cause. They did not want to admit that they were just a result. He told me who opposed public information about birth control and adequate medical treatment. The same ones who oppose decent living conditions for full term babies.

"I was impatient. I asked him, 'Why, but why?' He said, 'Good God, child, the poorer the masses, the cheaper you get labor and the stronger becomes capital.' But I said, 'The masses can go on strike. They're striking today, everywhere. I've read the papers.'

"Morck smiled. I didn't like that smile. He said, 'Yes, they can strike. Except for what it costs them to strike. Often their wages increase a little, then prices go up. Wages don't go any further than before. So they strike again. And the Last Holy Men can then wring their hands and point to the impossible workers: 'Look my friends, these greedy souls will never be satisfied.'

"The restlessness I'd been feeling was bothering me worse than ever. I wanted to go home. But I couldn't tear myself away. There were tears in my eyes when I said, 'Then it doesn't work. Then it'll never be any other way?'

"Morck got down off the table. He stretched. He said, 'Not necessarily, not necessarily. If wages can't increase without prices increasing, we have to figure out something else. So that wages increase and prices don't.'

"He said it with an expression that made me think he was making fun of me and of all the striking workers. But he laughed when he saw the expression on my face. He said, 'It's simple. Since it's impossible for those poor industrial lords to figure out this piece of arithmetic, then industry should change lords. Who can do it better.' I said, 'How? Who? What lords?'

"He placed himself directly in front of me. He was serious. He said, 'All those baby boys. Their fathers and mothers.'

"I said, 'Never again will I have it taken away. If a baby boy happens, I want him, no matter what. Even if I have to beg and receive child support.'

"My tears were running over and my hands were damp with this restlessness of mine. More and more strongly, I wanted to go home.

"But Morck held both my hands and stroked them to rest. He said, 'Go ahead. Then we'll have an increased slave market and even more people holding out their hats for a pittance against their dreary struggles, even more who'll increase their masters' wealth and their brothers' poverty.'

"I got angry. I almost lost my breath with anger. I tore my hands away from his and put my fists in my eyes to stop my tears. They were tears of anger. I said, 'Just because you're bitter. Just because you've lost faith and hope!' And I yelled at him, 'It's because you've failed. What have you done for your brothers?'

"I stopped there. I was stopped there by his eyes, by his face, pale as a corpse. Words were hanging on my lips, but fortunately they stopped there: And what have you done to your girl, to your child! Thank God, I didn't say it. I can't describe that face of his, with his pitiful blue and brown eyes. He was standing straight up and down, his arms hanging along his sides. He was swaying a little. I dried my eyes, blew my nose, and took my time about it. I didn't know what to do with my hands. God, how glad I am I didn't say it.

"He had turned his back to me and was drawing in the dust on the piano with one finger. After a long time he whispered—yes, he was almost whispering, but it was so quiet that every word sounded like the blow of a hammer. He said I was right. He had failed. But he said, 'A country's freedom is no less precious just because there are failures among those who fight for it. And the task before us is no less large just because some of us are insufficient and have betrayed the task.' And he said that children born to want and shame could not become happy human beings.

"*But!* If there were enough of them, if there was enough discontent and anger, then they would become the explosive charge that would blow up the mountain which blocked the road to a meaningful society.

"Then he looked at me and said, '. . . a society that greets all the baby boys in the world and that needs them and takes care of them, because it needs the strength and abilities of every human child who wants into this world.'

"He said a lot more that I don't remember. He riveted me with what he was saying, but I was alive with a creepy-crawly feeling of having forgotten something. I said, 'You must play for me again. Will you?'

"But he didn't want to. Not then. He said, 'I have a half bottle of liquor and I want to drink.' He asked me to leave. He wanted to be alone. He wanted to drink alone. But he held my hands when I was about to leave and promised he would play for me some other time. He'd let me know.

"That was that. When I got home I knew what it was that I had forgotten."

"The restlessness suddenly exploded in me. I knew what it was that I'd forgotten. My heart stopped beating.

"Because I'd forgotten—well, I'd completely neglected to pay attention to the last time I menstruated. It had been a long time ago. I remembered it now because I felt a tightening little ache in my breasts and an inkling of pain in my lower abdomen.

"My face got hotter. I had not had my period since before the time I spent with Johannes, that night when I came from Morck's. I was several weeks late.

"It is really strange what a sense of rhythm life has. For some of us. It plays with you, like a cat with a mouse, and hooks you with a claw every time you think you're safe, think you're all right. That's the way it's almost always been for me.

"Well, now the claw has come to stay, so now I can kiss all hope good-bye.

"You see, I'm going to die soon. It will be a long and painful death. And I have neither enough courage nor willpower left to help put an end to it. Did I tell you this? They told me today. Finally they told me the truth. This is the way they said it: 'You don't need to despair. Many people live for years and there may be periods without pain.'

"Well, well. There is nothing more that can be done about it.

"At the time I was just telling you about, my life had begun to take on some meaning. Maybe I could have amounted to something in life, something meaningful. I could see a glimmer, a hope of freedom.

"And then everything collapsed once more, in the blackest of despair. No glimmer any more, except for the one I tried to fabricate out of the darkness, almost hysterically.

"During the first few days I was thrown from one impossible state of mind to another. From a desperate hope that this could be wrong, a chance delay, the ache had just been a natural thing; it would come tonight, tomorrow . . . to a glowing hatred against everything and everybody, against Johannes, against myself. The hatred of hopelessness. I tried to put some order in my thoughts, to find a solution, find a way out. Take it away, get it over with. I needed money for that. Well, Johannes would have to give it to me. Would the doctor run the risk of a second time? Probably not. And I couldn't face going to Johannes. Nonsense. I'd have to commit the crime myself. Or else kill myself.

"Then there were moments when I just succumbed to despair and violent crying spells. Jealousy churned in me too; it ripped and tore worse than ever, particularly when I tried on the idea of going to Johannes, knowing he was a stranger to me now and that he was going to marry Svanhild in two weeks.

"Getting married! To Svanhild!

"Never. I raged. I was crazy with pain at the thought. I would prevent it; I would write her a letter to make her break with him immediately. I even sat down and wrote a letter to Svanhild, the pharmacist's daughter. God only knows what I wrote, but the pencil danced across the paper. There was a particular solace and satisfaction in delivering everything about Johannes and me in as bitter a way as possible. It made me lighter. I'd make a ruckus, I'd make them know I was around. I put the letter in an envelope, wrote her name on it and went to bed. And slept. And woke up early with the wildest misgivings. Hopelessness tore at me and pushed me up against a wall. The letter, the malicious vulgar letter, was like a nightmare weighing on me. I'd become this low, to the point of being vulgar and vindictive. Then I tore up the letter and cried and got sentimental and became fond of Svanhild at the thought of how much pain I could have inflicted on her. Svanhild was good, precious, beautiful and, truthfully, much too good for Johannes. Oh, God, how I sobbed and cried. I loved Svanhild. It's really true.

"I took particular care with the cleaning before noon. I'd become so terribly nice. I wanted to keep my child. Johannes and Svanhild would get it. She would probably love it as if it were her own because no one was as precious and wonderful as Svanhild. And I would be their housekeeper. I would peel the potatoes and do the wash and go through hell and high water for Svanhild and Johannes. I would not demand that my own child call me mother. I was washing and cleaning and dusting and emptying chamber pots in a fever. I'd found the solution; everything would be all right. I would go to see Svanhild as soon as I was done with the housekeeping and tell her, talk to her, tell her I loved her.

"I went to my room to wash my eyes and get dressed and fix myself up really nicely. While I was doing that, all my niceness left me and I became irate with hatred . . . what was Svanhild imagining anyway? That she could have both Johannes and the child while I slaved for them all? I was terribly ashamed about all that nonsense I'd been fantasizing about. I was seized by fury at those who were the reason, Svanhild and Johannes. Of course, I'd go see her. I would go at once, so that I couldn't change my mind. And she'd hear about what kind of woman she was. I would scream it at her so you could hear it all up and down the street. The whole town should know that that proper teacher and man on the council was expecting a child by me when he married her.

"I really went. I went with hot eyes and a cold nose, with knees that shook under me, down toward the pharmacist's house. Wouldn't you know she was in the garden, feeding the chickens, in a white dress and a little apron. She was calling 'chicachicadee' and scattering the corn. I stayed on the other side of the street. There was a little stairway with a wooden rail leading into a store that sold work clothes, wooden shoes, and wool yarn, and I held on to the railing as if I would fall at any moment. There I stood staring at her with hopeless admiration and burning hatred and a sentimental need to be her friend, seek her help, take her into my confidence. I smelled dinner cooking in all the houses and was following all her movements. I imagined her with Johannes. I looked at her soft arms, her hips, her breasts. My abdomen twisted with the pain of a knife turning. There she was clipping some roses and there I was freezing in the sunshine, holding my coat together at the throat, staring at her until I was ready to scream. She didn't see me. She didn't even notice me. She was bending and bowing down so that every line in her body stood out clearly under her light dress, and she was humming in a dark, slightly hoarse voice.

"Not until long after she'd gone back inside did I walk up to the store, deathly tired."

She got up and emptied the ashtrays. Then she opened the window and sat down on the windowsill. A pale sunlight completely erased her features; only the deep shadows around her mouth remained. The noise from the street was coming in. It was full morning and the time when most people went to work. I had work to go to too. But I didn't look at the clock. She closed the window, eliminating the street noise before she continued.

"A few days later, after what seemed to me years of hopelessness and desperation, I decided that I would look up Johannes, tell him how things were and without mercy demand that he take the consequences. No one other than he and I and the authorities concerned need know anything. He would have to contribute to the child's upbringing and help me get a job, preferably in another town. This was something I had to go through with.

"On the morning when I was lying there waiting for day to arrive so that I could go to Johannes early in the morning before he went to school, lightning struck me again. Well, I'd reached a kind of peace because I'd made some kind of decision, even though it was a bitter decision filled with fear and insecurity about the future, but a decision nevertheless.

"So there I was in bed letting my thoughts do battle with me.

"Then it came, a gray terror. It burst forth from some hidden place in my consciousness and spread out through my body until I lay there like a powerless bundle, feeling the cold eat its way from my feet upward.

"I hadn't given it a thought this whole time . . . I hadn't just been with Johannes. I'd slept with Mohn. In the course of a week I'd been with them both and during that time I'd not been menstruating.

"Well, I tumbled down a dizzying abyss as I lay there.

"I couldn't demand that Johannes be responsible.

"I couldn't demand that anyone be responsible.

"I didn't know who was the father of the child I was carrying."

◐

"Those first days following that panicky recognition come back to me as a poisonous grayish-yellow fog. I only remember bits and pieces. I think I tried to take my own life. I remember one day when a tremendous wind from the east was blowing. I know I was sitting on a steep rock by the sea and that seafoam was spraying my face. I remember the dizzying fear as I looked down. But I didn't dare. I talked to myself and was quite crazy. I raved and invoked all possible powers that be. I cried loudly and shamelessly. It was a good thing I was alone."

173

She slid slowly off the windowsill and came over to me. Without looking at me, she asked for a cigarette. There was a shiny gray dampness across her forehead. Her hands were so restless. They were in constant motion on the armrest when she sat down. It took a while before I could light her cigarette.

"I have to smile when I think about all the stupid things that are said about single women having or not having children. If anyone is of the opinion that any woman who wants children has the moral right to have them, The Just Ones say she should get married if she absolutely must have children. All you have to do is figure out how many men there are in this world, and how many women.

"Anyway, about a year after I got out of the clinic that time, I got married, properly and nicely. During that year I struggled to keep hunger away and my clothes together and to get a roof over my head. I kept to myself. I was scared to death. In addition, I'd been greatly reduced by the whole affair. I almost died from loss of blood.

"There was a lot of unemployment. You had to take what you could get and I took a job in a fish market. You know something? Every time I walk past a fish market and smell that particular smell of ocean-fresh fish and old fish blood that sticks to the floor, I automatically put my hands in my pocket and curl up my fingers. That's how cold my hands were during that time. There is nothing colder than fish and herring in the winter. I worked in a sweater and a jacket and a coat under the apron and big felt slippers on my feet. The cold flayed my hands and ached up through my arms. There is nothing colder than frozen herring. Andersen was a nice boss. He lived upstairs and invited me up to warm myself with coffee. I was more than grateful. He had a nice home. I'd never really been inside a nice modern home. Well, well. Nothing to go into now. We became friends. I didn't want anything else and he thought I was a very decent girl. He gave me gifts and invited me to the movies.

"Then we got married. I married Carl in order to live well, in order to always be warm and to never have to worry about whether or not I'd make it. He was nice, that's all I can say. He hit me a couple of times, but that was later. It was my own fault. It was about Johannes. Not only did I cheat on Carl but I gave Johannes money. It was the money that caused the whole thing to be discovered. But why am I telling you this now? Oh, yes, I was talking about women having to get married if we want children. Oh yes. And I wanted children. That was one of the things that enabled me to get over my aversion toward Carl. Did I mention this to you? He was nice; he was real handsome too, and I liked him well enough. But liking a man is not always the same as liking to go to bed with him.

"To tell you the truth, I've always been impressed with women who get married out of sensibility. Women who are much less experienced than I was when I got married, get married calculatingly, or sensibly, which sounds much nicer. It is a bit difficult, you know. It's strange that Carl didn't lose patience with me that first week. I was being childish and took to crying at the most inopportune moments. But it got better; it got much better later. If he had only wanted children right away I would still be married to him. Even a girl like me doesn't want to offend a child she's carrying or holding to her breast. But Carl was a careful man. It had to do with his store. He saved money and wanted to expand and become a rich man. His goal was to become 'a man of a hundred thousand.'

"What about Johannes? It was my fault. I wrote to him. There were some books I'd borrowed a long time ago that I still had. I just wanted to send them back to him, for the sake of orderliness. And I wrote a little letter to go along, telling him I'd gotten married, and so on. I got a letter back, a friendly letter. I kept it to myself. I had a good time with it and kept it a secret from Carl. It would be wrong to say that that's when I started lying to him, since I'd been lying to him the whole time, not telling him about myself, not mentioning a word about having been in the clinic after having mistreated myself so badly that I almost died. In order to get rid of a child whose father I didn't know. He didn't know anything about any of that. He gave me a sewing machine. I got an electric oven. He didn't know what nice thing to do next.

He was proud of me too. When we got married I was still very thin and impossible looking after my illness. I was straight-out ugly and to this day I don't understand why anyone wanted to marry me. I was so thin I had buck teeth from thinness. I'd gotten to look nicer after a while. I'd gained some weight because I had it easy and never needed to think about having to skip a meal or anything like that.

"Nevertheless, I wrote Johannes back one fine day, 'Thanks for your letter.' For a while we just corresponded, as friends. But such letter writing is dangerous. You wait for a letter; pretty soon you're only waiting for a letter. That's what happened to both Johannes and me.

"Johannes got the girl he wanted, the way it happens in novels. She was both beautiful and nice, naturally. There was nothing wrong with Svanhild. Johannes's mother lived in the town where I was married. She lived in the outskirts, in an area of rundown old buildings and stinking alleys. I looked her up. I wanted to see Johannes's mother. It was a part of him, a part of his childhood. I went to her home, said I came from such and such a town, that I knew her son, that I'd come to bring greetings from him. Nothing more. She talked about her son as teacher so and so. She showed me his and Svanhild's wedding picture.

"When I left her I understood why it looked from Johannes's letters as if he was not one hundred percent happy with Svanhild. Birds of a feather? There's something to that. There are certain things that are hard to adjust to. Someone who's always had a good life has difficulty understanding a lot of things. She was probably all right. And the working-class man who wants to climb the ladder has to get quite high to get rid of his working-class background. And Johannes had a weakness for women. He found solace in women the way others find solace in alcohol. Oh, well. He isn't free from the alcohol either. Mostly in the last few years.

"How did I get to talking about all this? It's difficult for me to concentrate on one thing at a time right now, you see. I know I have to leave soon and there's something I have to get rid of before I go.

"My marriage? It's so long ago, I'd almost forgotten it. I had a good life, very good. Got almost everything I wanted. But no children. My husband wanted to wait. He wanted me to buy myself a fur coat. He gave me five hundred kroner to buy myself a nice fur coat that I liked. But I didn't buy any fur coat. I hid the money, I wanted to wait and see.

"Once, when my mother was sick, I got to go home. It's true that I didn't think about cheating on Carl, who was so nice. This is really true. But I don't know, I did write to Johannes saying I was coming, saying I was staying in the new hotel in town. I told him that so he would know I was well enough off to live in a hotel, paying my way. I really thought that was why I wrote to him. After I'd been to The Mine and came back down to the hotel, he'd been there asking for me. It had been my intention to leave the next day. My mother was not so ill that I couldn't have left the next day.

"But I stayed. I thought maybe he'd come asking for me again, and if he didn't come I'd leave the day after. I wanted to see him, talk to him, say hello to him. After all those nice letters. Nothing more. I bought some cakes and ordered extra good coffee from the hotel kitchen. In case someone should show up. But I was thinking that if he didn't come I'd leave tomorrow. It didn't make any difference whether he came or not, but it would be nice. That's what I told myself.

"But I could neither read nor do a thing. I brushed my hair; I looked at the clock. And I had to wash my hands time and time again, they got damp so quickly.

"And then Johannes came.

"Oh God, this is difficult for me. You see, no, I don't think anyone can understand this. When there was a knock at the door I thought something would make me burst.

And then, there he was. Are you listening to what I'm saying? Johannes was standing in the door. He took off his hat and reached out a hand. My Johannes.

"Oh. How could I explain this to you. He'd gotten old. His face looked worn. He smiled. We were both almost shy with each other, but it was the old smile, a thousand stars in his eyes.

We stood there for quite a while, just looking at one another. Then he said something nice about my looks, but I couldn't say anything about his. I couldn't say anything at all, but I called for the coffee. Well, there was a long period of small talk about ordinary things and do you want a piece of cake and such. When he wasn't smiling there was this helpless look in his eyes that I recognized, that meant he was sad and not happy.

"I'll tell you, and I think this is true, if it hadn't been for the fact that his neck had become so small, so thin and strange, we probably would have parted like that; nothing more would have happened. I'm almost sure of it. His clothes had sort of gotten roomy for him. When I showed him the picture of her baby boy that my sister had given me, he had to put his glasses on. He looked old in those glasses. There was nothing for it. That neck. The skin in the palms of my hands was hungry to get rid of some tenderness. I had to touch his neck.

"Well, well. That was that. I stayed in town for another three days."

◯

"It was during the time that Johannes came south and tried to borrow some money that I gave him the three hundred kroner left from the money Carl had given me for the fur coat. I'd given two hundred to my mother. I thought I could probably get a fur coat for three hundred. But I gave the three hundred that were left to Johannes. Because there was something about a promissory note, and there was a lot of trouble in his marriage because of this money. She was used to the good life, you know. Always so nicely dressed. Then there was his debt from his student days. I couldn't stand seeing Johannes like that, so worried. Can't you understand that? We met. We were together, and I was always sort of full of stars inside when I met Johannes. I know it was a base thing to do, giving him that money, Carl's money. Johannes and I slept together, wherever we could. In empty lots after dark, in the park. Wherever it so happened. We met like criminals. It was an unadorned and naked relationship. But it tied us together. Oh, well, we'll never be free of one another. Because such things bind you. You become conspirators.

"I lied to Carl. I became disgustingly clever. And I became fond of him and warm toward him because he believed me. Can you believe we had a good life together? And yet, yet. If I'd wanted to excuse my behavior now, I would have said that I was not happy with Carl. But you should know how I was. That way you'll better understand that I left him because I had to. And the evil deed afterwards. That which I did to myself one more time. It couldn't be avoided.

"Yes, I had a good life with Carl. But. No one has been able to make me bloom, except Johannes. No one other than Johannes has lit a shower of stars in me, like an empty winter sky singing with silence and light.

"The fur coat, well. He asked, of course, how it was coming, Carl did. Then I was no longer so clever. When he asked me more closely he must have suspected something because I was no longer good at inventing things and felt myself going pale. I don't even remember it all. My memory is clearest about the time when he hit me the first time. It felt like a horrible cold thing in my face, like a sudden crookedness, and my surprise was bigger than anything else. And I thought, 'He bought me. He has bought me and paid for me and I have cheated him out of what he thought he bought, a woman to call his own.'

"It got nice once more. Well, . . . nice?"

She laughed without a trace of a smile in her eyes.

"Johannes had had some trouble with his wife, but she forgave him. They had a child and she was having another one. He was so happy he cried. He'd been drinking a little. He'd taken to drinking a bit, and he was so happy he cried because Svanhild wanted everything to be all right. I got a terrible letter from her. She knew about the times I'd come to town, pretending my mother was ill. It was all over town and everybody excused Johannes because I'd always been after him.

"Oh, well.

"Things were still all right with him and Svanhild when he was going to the town south of where I lived and wrote and invited me to come there. I found some excuse. It was easier to find an excuse now that I was not going to my own town, where Johannes lived. It was safe with Carl. He didn't know there was a teachers' meeting in that town. He thought all was well between us and didn't know I was sick with longing for Johannes.

"As I was walking down toward the boat, I changed my mind. It came over me suddenly. It was a raw, cold evening, a real blustery November evening. Carl asked my forgiveness for not accompanying me. He had some work to do at the store. There I was, knowing the store was bitterly cold. And then there was the fact that he had . . . well, it's almost nothing, but he'd put a bag of grapes in my suitcase before I closed it. The day before, I'd wanted to buy grapes. I wanted grapes that had just been delivered to the store, but they were expensive. Carl said we couldn't afford them. But he did . . . can you understand this? You have to understand what this means, that he had just bought expensive grapes for me and put them in my suitcase. Shyly. He did it so clumsily and didn't want me to give him a kiss. He went red then and said it was nothing.

"But I remembered it. I felt the cold and homeless roar of the fjord. I stood on the pier until the boat was gone and almost enjoyed freezing. I thought about Johannes and cried a little. I was through with Johannes then. I wanted an end to it; it was just too awful. I stayed until the lights from the boat had disappeared. Then I went home.

"It's strange that I should be telling you this. I hadn't thought I would tell this because you could get the wrong picture of Carl. But you have to remember how badly I'd behaved toward him, and remember that he'd gotten a pig in the poke, without throwing me out.

"So I went home. The store was dark. I was happy because I would find him at home. I wanted to tell him everything. I wanted to see if I couldn't be honest with an honest man and make something clean and whole out of it. And safe. Above all, something snug and secure.

"Well, I let myself in.

"I noticed it immediately, even in the hallway. It wasn't the same home. Maybe, without my perceiving it, there was a different smell. Or maybe I heard something, laughter. But I didn't recognize it. I just felt this pressure, you know, this restlessness, as if something bad was waiting for me. It had been a long time since I'd had that feeling. Mostly, I wanted to run away. But I didn't know from what. And I thought, I think I thought, 'Here's something you have to go through.' That's the feeling I had at any rate, when I walked into the living room.

"There I sat straight down. I was completely at a loss. My heart was beating my chest to shreds.

"There was a fire in the stove. It was nice and warm. But I was shaken through and through by seizures of cold. My teeth were chattering in my mouth. I recognized this. I'd been this way once before.

There was a half-empty wine bottle and three glasses on the table. Yes, three. Are you listening? There were three, and that was what had me at a loss. There were two women's coats in there, tossed over a chair. One of them had red fox on it; the other was quite wet and disheveled looking. I thought in my confusion that red fox wasn't rain gear. The bedroom was right next door.

She closed her eyes. Her hands were scratching the armrests. There was a slight shiver across her face. She slowly moved her mouth and shivered. I emptied my glass and lit a cigarette. She opened her eyes and looked at her glass but made no move to touch it. A peaceful look came over her face and she sat immobile, looking at her glass as she continued.

"The bedroom was just the other side of the living room. I heard everything. I was looking at a pillow I'd made for the sofa and loved it. But I heard everything. It was gross. I don't think I was jealous, but it was gross. I got nauseous. And I was a prisoner. If I'd been able to get up and leave, I wouldn't have been involved. But I could neither get up nor move. I couldn't even light a cigarette properly. I couldn't light it because my hand shook something terrible. I looked at the pretty lamp I'd bought recently. I'd wanted it and gotten it. It was a small part of my home. And I heard everything. Laughter, exclamations. Gross noises from a bedroom. I had to put out the cigarette. It made me nauseous.

"I suddenly couldn't stand it. I screamed.

"Yes, I screamed. It got quieter in there, but not completely quiet, not immediately. Then I screamed again. I'd stood up and was putting the whole back of my hand in my mouth to stop those screams but another one came, even though it had become utterly quiet in there.

"Then I sat down on the chair again. I thought I'd run away, but there I was, sitting on the chair. I thought I was about to have a big cry, but no crying came, not a tear. Just a frozen nausea.

"Carl had barely put some clothes on. I was overcome by disgust at the sight of him. Because his face was scared too. I had to look down at the table, I was so ashamed. I couldn't have been more ashamed had it been me caught in an embarrassing moment. In the park or something. Because everything is embarrassing and vulgar if you are caught. And Carl? He chose to get angry.

"Thank God, he chose to get brutal and awful.

"He called me the worst names. The women came to the door, and peeked. They were only half-dressed. They couldn't contain their curiosity; they had to peek at the door. Carl asked them to go to hell. Then they closed the door.

"God, it was awful. I don't remember everything. But I said nothing. They finally came to get their coats and Carl chased them out before they could get them on. He threw some money after them. It fell on the floor and the girls screamed that they didn't want any money, but in the nick of time one of them came back in like a little rat and scraped the money off the floor. And I don't know, but a sudden little flood came over my heart because she came back in and scraped up that terrible money in a hurry. Money she'd spit at him that she didn't want.

"It got quiet in our home after we heard the door slam.

"He said, 'You're probably leaving too?' I nodded. He turned his back to me and was crying. The worst part was what he told me then, when he'd gotten meek.

"Suddenly I threw up. I didn't have time to go anywhere or do anything about it. And I recognized this too and had experienced it before. But I couldn't remember when. Not until later.

"Carl poured himself some wine and drank. He said, 'I'll kill myself if you leave.' Then I told him. I told him that I'd left to do something awful and that I'd come back to make an end to all the lies and awfulness.

"The room smelled of vomit and wine. Neither of us did anything about it.

"At first he got desperate. I'd gotten completely calm after I'd said it. I got up to leave.

"At first he begged me. But I just grabbed my cap and started putting it on.

"When he realized I was serious, he went out of his mind. And then he hit me. I can still hear the sound of his blow and my own crying because it was terrible. But I've forgotten the pain.

"That was that. When I stood on the street, bleeding from my nose and mouth, I knew I'd burned my bridges. By then I'd told him that I'd never loved him and that he was right in calling me the names he'd used, because I'd sold myself to him."

She straightened up and wiped the dampness from her forehead with the little balled-up handkerchief. Then she put the glass to her mouth and drank, slowly and thoughtfully.

"Well, you know, it has happened since that I've sold myself, for a night. It has happened many times; for a while it happened

184

often. That was during the time when it was almost impossible to get a job. Even housekeeping jobs. You need references.

"You sell yourself for a night. It's a realistic trade. It isn't anything but what it says it is. And then you have the money you have to have in order to eat your first dinner in a week, or pay the rent.

"But marriage is a swindle because it's called holy. Yes, inviolate. Inviolate! Not least those marriages where there's a secret trade going on under a steady contract."

"Do you know what someone I once knew said to me one night? He said, 'Nothing grows by moonlight.'

"I got to thinking about that a while ago while the man I've loved all my life was snoring next to me. And I finally got so exasperated with myself and with him that I almost killed him.

"But it isn't his fault that I love him. He is all the strengths I've thrown away in my life. This is the reason people make such a mess of things, the reason they let the world go its own crooked

186

way and live in their own moonlight, not seeing, not wanting to see it: Moonlight is only a cold reflection of sunlight.

"I told you that I left my husband? He took it upon himself to hate me. When I asked him for help he showed me the door and said it wasn't his child. I discovered it a few days after I'd left. I was pregnant. And it was his. There had been just him for a while. But he didn't believe me. Didn't want to believe me because he hated me.

"I wanted to have the child. I was desperate after a while. I had not brought anything with me except some bare necessities, and I didn't own anything and nobody needed me. I cried in the street and talked out loud to myself because I was quite out of my mind during that time, hungry and angry. I wanted to break into houses, commit bank robbery, anything, because I did not want to do that thing one more time. I didn't want to ruin my body and soul one more time in order to kill the life that was growing inside me. I was willing to live with Carl again if he would take me in. But he wanted nothing more to do with me; he threatened court action. He would get the law on his side.

"And then I did it anyway.

"I did the same thing over again that I'd done at home that time, that I'd sworn I'd never do again, no matter what happened."

She had folded her arms across her lap and was leaning forward, rocking back and forth. She was clenching her teeth and breathing through them, trembling breaths of air.

"That other time was during the days when Johannes had taken out his wedding announcement and was marrying someone else. Did I tell you this? There I was, pregnant. By Johannes, I thought; ready to commit all sorts of mean things, threats of a scandal, anything at all to ruin or prevent that marriage. Because I wanted that child. But then I remembered that it was not necessarily Johannes's child. There had been someone else, a happenstance, a mistake made in despair. Someone named Mohn. Oh God, what a time. I went to the doctor, I begged him to help me,

187

but he didn't want to. He'd helped me once before; he didn't dare. I didn't know what to do; I knew so little about such things. I ran to my sister at The Mine to ask for advice because I knew she'd done it herself each time when they were broke. I went several times because, when all was said and done, I didn't dare say anything, after all.

"When I finally said it, there was a terrible scene. She'd completely forgotten that she'd been in the same situation, that she wasn't married when she had her baby boy. She married later and forced herself to do so.

"But she told me how to do it. I had to lie down then. I almost fainted."

She stopped and was biting her lip nervously. When she continued, it sounded as if she had difficulty talking. There was something pained and helpless in her eyes as they avoided mine.

"I did it only a few days later. Only then did I muster the courage to do it. And I will remember this all my life. It was the first time, but far from the last. And you must remember this! Because all those who say we don't deserve any better must know this, and all those who say there should be a punishment for such acts, in the name of morality, must know this. Punishment! Can you imagine? Punishment. After this. Good God.

"It was warm that day. Muggy and quiet. Gray, with a sickly yellow light in the sky. The birds were silent. The cat was whimpering and hiding, then fussing about, then hiding again.

"I was sitting in my room with sweaty hands. Then it got suddenly dark, with a heavy twilight. And then there was a shower. I moaned out loud with fear. The rain was hissing in the courtyard and pouring down the windows by the bucket. When it stopped, the sun came peeking out for a moment. It glittered in the raindrops trickling from the roof and dripping and weeping from the trees. Then it was dark again, a yellow darkness. Something rumbled far away, a low, ominous growl. Wildly, I thought, 'Now I'll do it.' But the murder weapon that was a knitting needle stayed on the table. I didn't dare touch it. Then there was a weak glimmer of lightning. I wasn't sure that it wasn't just something in my eye. It was quiet as death. Then I grabbed the knitting needle. I had to dry my hands. Drops of sweat were running down my temples. Then it growled again, the sound rose, the growling sprang loose from the horizon and flashed across the sky. Two sharp flashes of lightning, then a waterfall of rain. It clattered behind the mountain, reluctantly, subdued. It came like cannon fire, letting loose and being flung like flashing sheets of iron across the sky. There was a blinding light from a lightning flash, two flashes; then all hell broke loose. The sky exploded with a boom right above my head. The mountains on the other side of the fjord burst and collapsed. A thousand cannonballs fell and rolled around for a while across the earth made of iron. Lightning followed in their footsteps.

"I'd gotten one hand inside. The rest of my body was numb with fear. My tongue was without sensation and swollen in my throat. Nausea was sitting frozen in the back of my brain. The room was illuminated in blinding flashes, wiped away, and lit again. The white world was collapsing above me in a madness of noise.

"My fingers had gotten hold of something. It was without sensation. But pains of fear were flowing through my fingers, which had found the uterus opening. I snarled through my teeth, 'God, God, let the earth perish. Now I'll do it, now I'll do it.'

"I guided the knitting needle inside me and didn't know whether it was in the right place. Knitting needles cannot feel their way. I felt as if I was choking; my breath came in dry heaves. The thunder moved away a little, the lightning flashes came less frequently, and the rain drummed steadily against the window. I pushed with the knitting needle but felt nothing but resistance. I searched and searched with the weapon, but there was resistance.

"Then I set to. Drops of sweat ran down the bridge of my nose, and I noticed that I was sitting there with my tongue hanging out of my mouth. Because something burst. I could hear it inside my head from the soft crunch of tissues that burst. The pain ran along my spine and radiated across my loins and stomach. I screamed. I thought I screamed, but there wasn't a sound. More, more, push more, find another place. It had to be wrong. And I held the very tip of the weapon between my thumb and forefinger to find the opening to my uterus once more. It was difficult but I thought I'd succeeded. The steel needle slid a little heavily against something. It went far up. Then a piercing lightning of pain through my stomach, back and brain told me it had hit something. More, more, don't give up. Tissues burst. The sweat blinded my eyes. I heard a long rattling groan coming out of me while my hand let the weapon do its work with deranged courage.

"Then I couldn't do it any more. I was gasping for air. I heard the weapon fall to the floor. I heard the jingle with a jolt. I was exhausted and dissolving in tears and lay down across the bed to cry. But only dry gasps would come. I didn't have the strength to wash. After a while the pain quieted down. My body was one large fatigue.

"The storm had passed. I was completely indifferent to everything and I fell asleep then and there.

"You no longer look as if you need to sleep. You're not going to sleep either. This is what I want to tell you. People have to start being awake now and look around. This is what I want with you.

"On the morning after, something came out. I woke up from it; I thought it came out then. But it was just some bloody mucus. Don't squeeze your eyes shut, you must stand this. It didn't hurt particularly, during those few days. There was a constant, distant, and ominous pain following me everywhere; otherwise, I was just exhausted. On Saturday afternoon I just stayed in bed, and on Sunday morning I was in bed when there was a knock on the door. I mumbled, 'Come in,' indifferent.

"It was Morck. He asked if I was sick. But I was just tired. He said I had to hurry up and get dressed. I was going to church. Yes, it was strange. One of Morck's whims. He was crazy. I promised to hurry up. As he left he said that today was the day he wanted to play for me.

"Brilliant summer weather had arrived after the thunderstorm. It wasn't very far to the church, but it seemed like several miles to me.

"Well, how did all of this happen? I was steeped in my own thoughts. The sun was making diagonal beams all the way across the room out of the sparkling dust. There was a clearing of throats, sighing and coughing, a constant restlessness among the benches while pages were being turned in the psalmbooks. The voiceless mass of sounds billowed between the ceiling and walls of the church. A child talked loudly during the introductory ceremonies. The mother said, 'Ssshhh!' and the s whistled down from the vault. The subdued abdominal pains came through me in waves, and I was thinking my own thoughts. Psalm number so and so. Page turning and the clearing of voices. A prelude slowly started up. I was enjoying it with my eyes closed. My pains had become stronger. They were true menstruation pains. I opened my eyes and listened to them and the music. The altarpiece lay in the shadows. It was blind behind a broad diagonal beam of slowly floating sundust. Only the red color shone through. I was thinking my own thoughts and noticing that my pains were coming alive. The organ music was slowly running up and down the whole register. I thought with a tender little pleasure that he was playing for me. My pains began to flare up.

"The tiny little moment of silence before the psalm starts had arrived. In that flash I saw the face of Christ. It was just for a split second while a few specks of dust died down; then they came back and blinded the face once more. But in that second it shot into my consciousness and stayed there, quivering, this glance toward the pulpit of suffering exasperation. The pain raged through me in waves. And the music began.

"Well, you almost have to have experienced this.

"Some people had started singing too, but they stopped, uncertain and out of order. They looked at one another. They turned toward the choir.

"A few chords broke loose from up there; they grew into a mighty column that stayed there, roaring.

"Then a storm broke over the church. Yes, the storm from that

191

past night broke loose above the unsuspecting church sound. I tried to stand up but had to sit down immediately. I sank down with a little groan. It came from the walls and the ceiling, a furious, flaming ocean of music. The church was on fire.

"Serious little Sexton Holmsen disappeared. The minister was standing at the pulpit, tense, caught off guard and frozen to the pulpit. People got up and sat down. The music rose and sank, a resounding red victory banner, a doomsday.

"All at once it was quiet. The restlessness, the whispering and mumbling sounded like the waves on the beach after a warship has passed, and the *s*'s whistled up toward the vault. You could hear voices coming from the choir, an agitated man's voice; then that got quiet too.

"The organ shut up. Sexton Holmsen came back in a hurry. The church was utterly silent. On a timid sign from the sexton, the minister came down. They whispered and whistled together.

"The minister knelt down in prayer in front of the altar for a moment. Then he turned toward the breathless congregation and cleared his voice.

" 'You must sing the psalm without the organ. The organist is . . . hmm. Unwell. Yes, dear members of the congregation. God's punishing hand has touched our organist. Let us pray for him.'

"And then the minister very nicely bowed his head and prayed for the strayed organist, Morck, and prayed that he would be converted and forgiven and find the grace of God. And the churchgoers were standing with their hands folded and their heads bowed.

"Except me.

"I sat, feeling that something was coming, a slow warm stream. But I didn't bow my head and I didn't fold my hands. I wanted to leave at once. I wanted to run after Morck and follow him home. But I could not move.

"The song sounded so touchingly brittle and ready to burst with loneliness in that big room without an organ. It put a pale hue of blind confidence where Morck a moment earlier had lit a blazing fire of a revival speech that no one but I had understood.

"But I understood him! And it was for me, for me, for me he had shouted this call, his very last, desperate call.

"Because that was the end. I didn't see him again.

"I stayed there alone, while the congregation dragged, creaked, and shuffled out. It lasted forever. My clothes were ruined by then. I couldn't show myself to anyone. My pains were sucking at me and waves of warm blood were pouring out of me. I finally got out of the empty church, without Sexton Holmsen noticing. There were tracks wherever I went, red tracks on the holy floor of the church.

"I sneaked down between the graves and hid in the toolshed. I put the hook on the door and stayed there until dusk arrived in the evening. I sat on the floor with chattering teeth, quietly moaning. I kept it in my handkerchief. I had gathered it up and hidden it inside my handkerchief.

"It wasn't big. No more than a slimy lump of blood that smelled bad. Nevertheless, I thought my stomach, my brain and my heart and everything, would be driven out of me when it came.

"You aren't sleeping, are you? No, you mustn't.

"Half crazy with pain and my face frozen with tears, I buried it. I found a poor, neglected grave with a crooked wooden cross with a tin sign where the name was almost erased. You could only read, 'With Faith in her Saviour' and the first name, 'Marie.'

"That's where I buried the tiny, little fetus."

She was sitting there looking down while her fingers clutched and clutched at the little handkerchief. Her hair had become stringy and messy. There was something disheveled in her face. Her eyes closed continually and her head sank down from its own weight. She straightened up again and looked at me with a burnt-out glance.

"That was that.

"I got sick. It wouldn't stop. And I heard that Morck was being fired.

"At night I stole empty bags from boathouses, old newspapers, whatever I could find. For bedding.

"But one night I pulled myself together and went to Morck's. It was Thursday, I know that because it was the day before I came down with a fever and was sent to the city. He hadn't lit a light. But it was a bright summer night, and it could have been that. . . .

"It smelled badly in the hallway upstairs. A slow stinking silence, a silence without breath. The door was locked from the inside. I shook it. I beat on it, but my beating only gave a dead echo and I didn't dare hear my own voice, didn't dare call his name. I whispered it between my teeth. That silence! And I knew.

"I ran down into the street. I knocked on the first and only door. I didn't go back up. The sheriff came and the door was broken open.

"Morck had cut his wrists many days earlier."

She had leaned back and closed her eyes. Her mouth was half-open, and her face caught the sallow light of day. She slept.

It was full day outside, with all its gray song.

I must have slept a little anyway.

I was sitting with my head in my hands, and when I looked up there was no one in the chair where she had been sitting. There was no one in the room but me. A bitter cigarette smoke hung in the air, leftovers from the night. I was shaking with cold.

She wasn't in the kitchen. She was nowhere in the apartment. She was gone. Her suitcase was gone.

I couldn't call out for her because I didn't know her name.

I've looked for her for thirteen days now. I've crisscrossed the city. I've been everywhere. I've walked around the railroad station for hours; that's where I met her that evening. There isn't a place I haven't been during these thirteen days, looking for her blue coat.

But I haven't found her.

Not yet.

Torborg Nedreaas, a Norwegian author of international renown, was born in Bergen, Norway, in 1906. She died in June, 1987. Her reputation as a national literary treasure was recently acknowledged by the publication of her collected works.

Before and during World War II, Nedreaas made her living writing short stories for weekly magazines. The best of these were published in 1945 under the title *Før det ringer tredje gang* (Before the Third Ring), but her literary debut is more properly recognized by *Bak skapet står øksen* (Behind the Cupboard Stands the Ax), a collection of short stories published that same year, all of which describe the war and its effects on everyday life. Many of these stories are about young Norwegian girls who were seduced by the excitement and brutality of the German occupation forces, only to have their heads shaved by the victorious heroes of Norway.

Av måneskinn gror det ingenting (Nothing Grows by Moonlight) (1947) brought critical acclaim and recognition. A vehement indictment of male power, individual as well as political and social, it was a work ahead of its time. Reprinted in 1981 and adapted for the stage as a one-woman play in early 1982, it is enjoying wide popular success.

Postwar Norway, caught in the throes of the international cold war, is the subject of *De varme hendene* (The Warm Hands) (1952). Panned by most critics, it was not published in paperback until twenty-one years later, when a new generation of readers, with a different view of the world, appreciated its antimilitarist social and political stance.

Trylleglasset (The Crystal Ball) (1950) and *Stoppested* (The Stop) (1953), both collections of short stories, introduce the reader to

Herdis, the young girl who is the main character of *Musikk fra en blå brønn* (Music from a Blue Well) (1960) and *Ved den neste nymåne* (By the Next New Moon) (1971). The setting for all the stories about Herdis is the pre–World War I neighborhood where Nedreaas grew up, one in which upper-middle-class, white- and blue-collar workers, and the poorest of the poor live in close proximity. Herdis, an only child often excluded from play with other children, seeks solace in a crystal ball that changes the world and makes it beautiful. Symbolically, the crystal ball stands for the artistic and literary development of the main character. The pitfalls and elations of artistic development are a recurring theme in Nedreaas's writing about Herdis, fully explored and incisively described in *Musikk fra en blå brønn* and *Ved den neste nymåne*.

Between the publication of those two novels a collection of stories called *Den siste polka* (The Last Polka) (1965) was released. Many of these stories deal with the mechanics of everyday life taking priority over larger, more important social issues.

I det blå (Out of the Blue) (1967) is a collection of essays previously broadcast for Norwegian Radio. In addition, Nedreaas has written six plays for radio and television.

Over the years Nedreaas's work has been translated into fourteen languages, reaching a broad readership. Her last novel, *Ved den neste nymåne,* was published in the Soviet Union in an edition of 1.5 million copies, and in 1982 *Musikk fra en blå brønn* appeared in France, where it received the Prix Kaminski-Halperine for the best foreign translation.